I0772619

Contents

Session #1

D EAR DR. AARON RUTLEDGE,

This is not an easy story to tell, and I am so thankful you're willing to listen.

Where to start?

I guess I should start with the horrific day that changed everything.

I was in the library with my psychology class. I had just grabbed my hair and was pulling at it, looking at the disorganized mess of notes in front of me. We were working on a project, making flashcards of famous figures; I was assigned Sigmund Freud. And, if I remember correctly, he was a big proponent of talk therapy. Ironic, huh?

That's when it happened. Our principal's voice came over the intercom. In the coldest and most emotionless voice I've ever heard, he simply said, "Lockdown. Not a drill."

A switch flipped in my brain. My heart jumped into my throat, and air rushed out of my lungs. Blood drained from my teacher's face. Already in action, Ms. Mullen, the librarian, dashed over to the lights and switched them off.

It was happening. We had trained for this. *Run, Fight, Hide.* I didn't need to hear my teacher's instructions before I dove under a nearby table. It was instinct. My fight-or-flight response controlled my every move. A moment later, I heard screaming and popping sounds in the distance. I froze—completely immobile.

Time froze, too. Everything happened quickly but strangely took forever, like when you leap into the deep end of a pool. It's like you're floating for a second. You wonder if gravity stopped working. Then, time speeds back up as you splash everything around you.

As I sat under the table, he popped into my thoughts. His face, his smile. I wondered if he was safe. I wondered if *I* was safe. My breath quickened, and a tear worked its way down my cheek. Take some breaths, I told myself. But I couldn't. That's fight or flight for you.

The screaming grew louder. Frantic footsteps followed. More gunshots sounded in the distance. My mouth dried up. My heart fluttered in agony. My chest tightened, and it felt like I was attempting to breathe through a straw. My mind raced. *Are we safe? Was the library safe? Who is screaming? Why is this happening?* In the distance, someone screeched obscenities, and I could have sworn I heard thuds on the ground.

Something slammed into the library door. Whatever it was tugged at the handle. My heart pounded against my ribs. My mind returned to his face. The door opened.

"Quick, come in!" Ms. Mullen exclaimed. More screaming assaulted my eardrums, and the door slammed.

Whoever just entered the library made a gut-wrenching sound of death that filled the room. At first, I couldn't look. The voice told me everything I needed to know.

I thought about God. My next thought was a furious plea: why would you do this? After everything, why?

"We need to stop this bleeding," Ms. Mullen said flatly.

"Too...much," the voice cried out.

I forced myself to look, perhaps against my better judgement. I don't want to get into what happened next. I'm not sure I can bring myself to say it, and you did say that we didn't need to talk about anything that I wasn't comfortable with right away. It all gets a bit hazy, too. I remember the crimson stains. His blood soaked the librarian's floral shirt and the outdated green carpet. I remember the yelling. I remember the tears. I remember the silence when the screaming stopped...when he met Saint Peter.

Fifteen students died that day. Many more were injured.

It's still hard for me to think about the shooting, but my brain refuses to give me a break from the memories. They haunt me. I continually relive the horror. The popping sounds still echo in my mind.

School is where we should feel safe—where we focus on learning, growing, and preparing for the future.

That future was cut far too short. I feel helpless, but I am also pissed! I am so angry it happened to us. My blood simply boils that we had to experience it—people offered their thoughts and prayers and then moved on like nothing happened. They pray to make themselves feel better about doing nothing—absolutely nothing—to make changes.

My life is a void now. All I can do is think about it. The images of that fateful day replay in my mind like they're on a loop: when I want to sleep, when I am at the store, when I watch television. I smell the blood. The screams call to me. The ghosts of the massacre haunt me. Whenever I think about it, I freeze. I sweat. A lump forms in my throat. I tense up, and I zone out. It repeats, again and again. Whenever I feel I am making progress, I am thrust back into the library. I am back, hearing the screams turn into sobs and then into nothingness.

I hope as we talk about my story, I can move beyond the death and pain. I don't know what that looks like yet. But I want to find something else. I want to find joy, hope, and happiness again. I've walked through the valley of the shadow of death for long enough, and I want to traverse different terrain. I desperately want that.

It's been over a year since the shooting, and I am still struggling. So, I have come to you. I must admit this: I avoided seeking you out for a long time. I don't really want to share much with you, but I also know that not talking is not helping at all. I am so thankful you're going to listen to my story and help me process...well, everything. I'm glad you told me to write everything down in your welcome email. Right now, after writing, I'm feeling...better, more in control, like the ink is all the toxic energy draining out of my body.

Session #2

DEAR DR. RUTLEDGE,

At the end of our last session, you said something about finding something to do, something fun, something to force me to get up and get moving.

That's what I did this week. I thought of something I hadn't done in a long time. Walking in nature raised my spirits like the Christmas present you looked forward to the most, or at least it used to.

I took a bit over an hour to drive to Presidio Park. I turned down the familiar dirt road and parked. My car was the only one there. I had the trails to myself. Once out of my car, I took a deep breath and breathed in the crisp, clean air. The park always had a stillness to it, like time would just stop when you were there.

I started my journey to my favorite overlook. I took my time and soaked in nostalgia as I recalled the smells, sounds, and sights. The crisp smell of pine. Bird's chirping without a care in the world. All the lush vegetation. This hike had always been a happy place for me. I marveled at how still and calm the trail always felt, even with the birds chattering, squirrels dashing from tree to tree, and rabbits ducking for cover as soon as you saw them.

Eventually, I arrived at the overlook. This cliff always provided a marvelous view of the forest as far as I could see. Peaceful, that's how I described it. In an instant, the overlook always reminded me how beautiful and vast the world is.

Not a cloud in sight. I sat a couple of feet from the edge and soaked in the sun. The rays of light felt so good on my skin. I couldn't help but smile at the heat I felt.

The warmth of the sun and the stillness of the forest engulfed me in an embrace, and I felt alive. I reflected on what I was feeling and my emotions. The smile on my face told me that I felt good—really good—for the first time in a while. But a twinge of pain in the pit of my stomach remained. Oddly, my chest started to tighten up, too.

I exhaled. Of course, the moment was bittersweet for me. I thought back to the time I brought Mario up here.

Mario...

I'm sure we will be talking about him during our sessions for a long time. For now, I'll say that the pain of losing him was still with me—is still with me.

Yet, in that moment, I tried to pay attention to both emotions: feeling good but hurting, too. A tear formed in the corner of my eye as I realized I was feeling something. I had been so numb for so long that just feeling anything was a tad overwhelming—but in a good way, I think.

As I walked back to my car, I realized another thing.

I wanted to live. I was just in a place where I could have jumped, but I didn't. I could have ended it, never having to feel the pain again. But I didn't. I didn't want to. I wanted to stay alive, and it is strange to say that I surprised myself. Just below all that numbness was a deep desire to fight, to live, to feel good again. For so long, I hadn't felt like I was living. Or maybe it's better to say that I was living to avoid pain. I wasn't living to be happy.

But there, at Presidio Park, I knew with all my being that I deserved happiness and wanted to feel joy—that kind of joy that just makes you feel like your chest is so full of love that you are surprised you don't burst. I want that bliss that makes you wonder why you haven't started floating.

I know that this will be a lot of work. Healing is a difficult journey. But I deserve it. I've been numb for almost as long as I can remember, and now I deserve to feel the warmth again.

Session #3

Dear Dr. Aaron,

I haven't wanted to talk about this, but I know it is necessary. I must rip off the band-aid to heal in a healthier manner.

I'm afraid to love again.

When I filled out that intake form or whatever to start seeing you, it asked what my goals were. I guess one of them is to learn to love again. I feel on guard all the time, never letting anyone in. And I don't want to live this way forever, but I'm so deadly afraid of opening myself up to more heartache.

I guess since that's my goal, I suppose we should talk about him for a bit, too. His name was Mario Sanchez. He was one of the fifteen. Mario loved his sports. He made the varsity basketball team as a sophomore. I know he would have led the team to a state championship or something...if he had been around for our senior year. The team had already voted him team captain as a junior. I think that was the first time it happened in the whole history of our school. He was pretty darn smart, too, working to make sure he could get a scholarship for sports or smarts. He had the most infectious smile and laugh. He lit up the room. And he was not like the other jocks. He cared about everyone. He would help people with their Spanish homework and quiz them on their vocabulary, although he would get annoyed with those requests from time to time. He was human, after all. We had this shy girl in one of our classes, and others would tease her. Our English teacher mentioned that she had autism to me one time. Mario never made fun of her, even when others did, and he would invite her to join his groups in class. His smile somehow always ended up on her face. He just loved people and wanted everyone to experience joy and happiness. He was always there if you needed someone to talk to. He enjoyed iced toasted marshmallow lattes. I didn't even know there was such a thing until I met him. He deserved so much better. We all did.

I loved him. We were partners. Like boyfriends. No one else knew. In fact, you are the first person I have ever told. I mean, we had talked about coming out to everyone. But we lived in a conservative area. Every election year, signs for Republicans appeared on every street. We constantly would hear homophobic things at school: "Liking it in the rear makes you queer." Horrific things like that. We kept saying things like we would wait for college to announce our relationship to the world. We had this beautiful future planned. Well, I guess I should say I had crafted this image in my mind of how we would live this wonderful life, as they say, happily ever after. I never told Mario all the details. We would go off to some big city and go to college together. We would be out. We would go on dates—in public! We would live together. We would buy a house and adopt two and a half shelter dogs if we decided not to have kids. We would be the power couple that we could never be in high school. We would be...free.

In some ways, I still feel like I am living a lie because I have never talked to anyone about what we were. And what we were is still a huge part of me. But it is still not my secret to share. It is his. That's how I've been thinking about it anyway. I find myself caught in this space where I feel the urge to talk about him and how much I still love him and want to honor his wishes of waiting to share our relationship with others. Yet, because his life was cut short, it is so hard to bring it up to others, and I really do not want to. What if it hurts too much to discuss? Will it re-traumatize me? Maybe they will think I am making it up? Maybe it is still his secret to share? I don't know. I can never make sense of what I should do about it.

That's probably another reason I've come to see you. I need to learn how to navigate these thoughts, and I need to find some peace as my mind wars with itself.

I hesitate to share my story with you and with others. I want to share my story in hopes that it will help someone someday, but I honestly wonder if it will do more harm than good. I am sick and tired of all the movies and television shows that just kill off queer characters. Most queer characters never make it past season two. I do not want to bury any more queer characters, and I frankly struggle with my emotions when I encounter yet another story of queer death. The trope is overused and cliche. I hate it, and it's just awful. But what if your story is one of queer death? What if you hate your story because death occupies so much of it? What if that death shaped who you are, and you find it impossible to tell your story without talking about it? Around every turn and plot point in my life, death still lingers with me. I desperately wish that I could tell a different story, but sadly, that's not my story.

Session #4

Dear Aaron,

I've been thinking a lot about how everyone used to call me a good Christian boy. I loved singing in church. I knew all the motions to each song, and I exaggerated them beyond belief. We had this one song where you would pretend to shrink to the ground; strange, I know. And I would basically be lying on the floor by the end of the verse. I always knew all the answers in Sunday school. I memorized all the verses.

But I doubt they would call me a "good" Christian anymore, especially if they ever learned what Mario and I felt for each other.

Christians can say the most hurtful things. The hardest place to find God is inside the walls of a church. At least, that's what I find when I attend a service. Of course, my mind thought about a myriad of different things the first time Mario graced the sanctuary.

A few weeks before the start of sophomore year, Mario's family moved to town and started attending our church. They came in a little late and sat down a few rows in front of my family. As soon as I saw his curly, dark brown hair, I was fixated. I could not stop looking at him except for when I looked to see if others noticed how much I was staring. Who knows what the sermon was about? Not me. It was probably another lecture about how society is becoming too sinful. I hated those sermons. The God I know cares and loves. My God is a different God to the one others profess to believe in. Sitting in pews suffocated me. I felt isolated as they worked to confine the infinite beauty of God's creation in this dull, little box. Pleased with themselves for going about life in the "appropriate" manner, they condemned those who lived and loved differently.

Fast forward to Wednesday's youth group meeting. I enthusiastically looked forward to it for weeks. We planned on attending a huge youth ministry program in Big Rapids. That night, Mario and I heard many toxic and venomous words. It was then I first decided I needed to talk to him. That night, I felt like I knew him and that he would know me.

Before hitting the road, we scarfed down dinner, pizza, and some salad. I grabbed a slice of pizza when I heard a new voice. A little startled, I looked over and saw him. At first, I noticed his smile. Simply gorgeous. I don't know how to explain it best, but it was like his smile somehow formed on my face. It was infectious. I just stared at those pearly whites. My mouth dropped in awe. He walked with such confidence. I wanted to go over and introduce myself, but I hesitated. Unsure of myself, I took a bite of my pizza and immediately felt some of the sauce splatter on my chin. Of course, I would get sauce on my face when I was trying to make a good first impression! At that time, I already knew I was gay. I had not told anyone except for my dog and God. I did not know it then, but I wanted to impress my first and only boyfriend. What I would not give to experience my heart racing from being around him one more time.

We loaded into two large passenger vans and drove forty-five minutes to Big Rapids. Several other youth groups piled into the massive auditorium. The atmosphere was electric, and the hairs on my arms swayed along with the movement of the van; I knew the night would be deeply moving and transformative.

It was. At least, at first, it certainly did not end that way. It ended in pain, especially for me. I honestly do not remember much about the evening. I do remember one moment, forever seared in my memory.

The featured pastor was a woman. I don't really know if it matters. Maybe it is because I generally associated women with being more welcoming, but that was probably just a stereotype that I needed to unlearn. Because this woman was anything but welcoming.

She delivered a moving sermon about how Jesus Christ died for us all—how He had taken lashes for each of our sins. As she spoke, she crafted an unforgettable visual of what Jesus "suffered for us all." She had brought a horsewhip, and she slashed the air with it as she listed several sins: pornography, infidelity, and gluttony.

But then she arrived at me.

"The sin of homosexuality!" Cue more cracks. She must have left marks on the stage. That whipping sound assaulted my ear and my soul.

My heart sank as she delivered what felt like a fatal punch to my solar plexus. I suddenly gasped for air. I felt betrayed. I can still hear the venom in her voice. Were all these feelings I had really so wrong? A knot formed in the pit of my stomach. I almost heaved. I began to release a deep breath but snatched it back in case anyone noticed. Her words stung as if I had been lashed with her whip. I did not want anyone to know how much pain I suddenly found myself in.

I looked over the rest of the group to see if anyone was watching me, but my gaze rested on Mario. His lips seemed tense; his earlier smile was gone. His brow furrowed. His eyes glistened. Was he on the verge of crying? It certainly looked like it. Somehow, I knew he was in pain, too. My arm muscles tensed. My chest tightened. The knot forming in my stomach turned into anger. My jaw clenched as I scowled at the preacher. My body decided fighting was preferable to flight. How could anyone who claimed to follow Christ cause what I just saw on Mario's beautiful face? It was then I decided I needed to talk with him, but I just did not know how. I'd never been a timid child by any definition, but navigating my sexuality promoted a whole new level of unfamiliar anxiety. And this was not something I wanted to mess up.

On the ride home, so many of the others seemed overjoyed with our joint experience. It was certainly persuasive. You couldn't help but feel the electricity circulating around the auditorium. For me, the energy became an annoying buzz as we drew closer and closer to home. I noticed Mario was as quiet and solemn as I was. When asked, we both simply said we were feeling tired; it was, after all, long past our bedtimes. It was not a lie; my body ached, and my mind kept going blank. I just wanted to escape into sleep.

For the rest of the evening, my mind raced in a vain attempt to process what happened. The hurt from her yelling about the sin of homosexuality. Mario's face and whether we had been feeling the same thing.

I never want anyone else to have that expression. No one should have to experience such pain. During an earlier session, you asked me about what I wanted in life and what I wanted to get out of our sessions. I want to ensure that other Marios out there never have to feel what we felt. I doubt I'll ever succeed, but I want to try. I want to feel confident in myself and in my ability to defend myself and others.

I want to learn how to use the pain of my past as a blessing for those in the present. I want that more than anything.

Session #5

HI Aaron,

I'm still thinking a lot about Mario.

After seeing the hurt on his face, I spent the rest of the week agonizing over how to bring it up with him. Whenever I planned the conversation in my head, I remembered how awful it would be to discuss it all at church. What if someone overheard us? What if he immediately went to the pastor? What if I misread the situation? What if he wasn't gay? Would he want to talk? Would he spread rumors about me? What if he was about to cry because he was happy that she was attacking queer folks? I doubted that last thought, but the questions bombarded my mind all week until Sunday's church service.

I took a few breaks from gazing at him to listen to the sermon. Thankfully, we were still on our break from fire and brimstone. You can't call out the same sins every week; things would get boring. This week, one line caught my attention. "Find people you can trust and build faithful relationships with them." That was it—trust. I wondered who I could trust with my sexuality. Who would be willing to have a serious and loving conversation about this? Who could I come out to? My parents? Mario?

After the service, the congregation always rushed off to the fellowship room, where everyone talked about their week. The church felt close. I knew I belonged there, at least until I came out to myself. The fellowship room smelled of recently brewed coffee, which called my name, as did the several packets of sugar that I poured into my cup. I grabbed a chocolate chip cookie, too and stood to one side by myself.

Mario had all the courage in our relationship. I did not wait long for him to approach me as I was eating the cookie and, of course, getting crumbs all over my shirt. Have I mentioned I'm a messy eater? It's a prominent feature of who I am.

"Hey, Jason, right?" he asked cautiously.

"Yeah, that's me," I replied. My heart loves to race, mostly from anxiety. It likes to pound away in my chest anytime I do anything that could be considered slightly awkward. At any rate, my body pulsated with a strange mixture of nervous energy and excitement. I was talking to him.

"I'm Mario. I just wanted to introduce myself," he said.

"Nice to meet you, Mario," I said, brushing off cookie crumbs on my pants leg before reaching my trembling hand out towards his.

Time slowed. A magnetic energy guided our hands together for the first time. His hand was firm but softer than I guessed. Something inside me approved of this touch because all the nerves in my hands lit up instantly. A warm, almost electric, current ran up my arm. My body yearned for more, a hug, a piggy-back ride, to hold on longer, literally anything. Sadly, our hands released as he continued, "So, you know, I'm new to town, and I want to start introducing myself to new people."

"Oh?"

"Yeah, I want to feel at home here, you know?" he asked.

"I can imagine. This can be a lonely place if you don't know anyone," I replied.

"Oh yeah? Why is that?" he asked as his eyebrows quizzically furrowed.

I let out an awkward laugh, "Well, as you may have noticed, there is just not much to do unless you go to Big Rapids."

"I sort of got that feeling," Mario stated. "Luckily, I play basketball, so hopefully, that will keep me busy."

"Really? From what I hear, our basketball team could use some good players," I joked.

"Well, hopefully, they will let me on the team," he replied, perhaps unaware of how truly awful our high school basketball team was. "I want to make varsity this year."

"I'm sure you will," I said with another chuckle.

"You haven't even seen me play yet," he replied.

"I'm not sure I need to," I laughed again. He seriously had no idea how often the team lost.

"Well then, I guess I do have that to look forward to," he said with a little smirk.

"I would bet on it," I said. "Even in church."

"Take it we don't believe in gambling in this church?" Mario questioned.

"Oh, it is not a gamble at all," I replied, surprised at myself. Usually, I struggle to keep a conversation going. Or maybe I was being so awkward that I felt like it was going well?

And just like that, I overthought everything. Cue a moment of awkward silence. How did this always happen to me? I just smiled a let out a little exhale, waiting for Mario to save us and our conversation.

"Well, I wanted to ask if you wanted to meet up sometime?" he asked, "You know, help me get to know the town a little more."

"Yeah, sounds great," I responded with probably too much enthusiasm. I prayed I didn't appear desperate.

But he reacted smoothly. "Okay, cool! Maybe we could meet up before youth group?"

"Sounds good to me. Let me give you my number," I said as I looked around for some paper to write on. It took me a moment, but I scribbled my number down and handed it to him. After we said our goodbyes, I eagerly waited for Wednesday to arrive. The nervous energy stayed with me all day on Monday and Tuesday, but it strangely felt good—as if something magical was about to happen.

Session #6

HEY AARON,

I know we've been talking about my relationship with Mario, and I do want to talk about it more. I feel like saying everything out loud will help me process it all, but, as you can imagine, my mind has been...distracted.

It all started after I heard about the latest school shooting. This time, the halls of Bay City High School echoed with the sound of an AK-47. I had never heard of the school before, but now I knew I'd never forget its name. Shootings never fail to resurrect the pain. I feel this weird mix of emotions—anger, sadness and hopelessness. My blood boils, and I just want to cry. It certainly is not my favorite feeling, but I have been working on channeling these feelings into something positive. So, this past week, I went to my first protest. Last week, you mentioned something about the importance of finding community; I wanted to give it a try.

My strange mix of emotions followed me to the march, and tears worked their way down my face multiple times. But other emotions joined the anger, the sadness, and the hopelessness. I remained pessimistic about everything, but I felt hope trying to creep its way into my heart. The march affirmed me and my experiences. I saw all the people who are working for a better world, and it made my world a bit brighter, even if only fleetingly. Even if nothing happens and the cycle of inaction continues, I am glad I got to bask in that light for an afternoon. All the people there were worried about gun violence, and we need to show each other we are not alone. Our presence always matters, even if it does nothing to address the epidemic of gun violence.

We met on the lawn of the city courthouse for speeches before we marched to City Hall. The buildings are only a mile away from each other. Fortunately, it was sunny and warm. The cheery weather contrasted sharply with the somber tone. The speeches got to me, especially when they listed the names of people murdered in the recent shooting. I cried. This time, the speaker also announced the names of the students who died in my school. I don't know what is worse: hearing the names of the students and the memories flooding back, or not hearing their names and wondering if people have forgotten about the lives lost that day. I said a silent prayer for the fifteen as the speech continued. When I prayed for Mario, his smile momentarily appeared on my face as I thought about how wonderful he was. But the smile left with haste. *How many other folks here knew and lost someone to gun violence?*

I struggled to listen to the speeches, but they certainly moved me. Strangely, they simultaneously drained me and energized me to fight for change. Speakers talked about their fears for their children attending school. They called for action: for background checks. One of the speakers talked about how he enjoyed hunting but also wanted to make it safe to visit shopping malls and movie theaters. His shirt read, "Hunter for Gun Safety." Others repeated some of the cliché lines like "their thoughts and prayers are not enough" and "we are the only country in the world that faces this issue." I do not mind those lines. But they felt hollow. Nothing ever happens after people use those lines.

Another speaker talked about how he lost his mother to gun violence. That was powerful. The love and hurt poured out of him with every word. It was when I thought most about Mario. I wanted to jump on the stage and yell about how I had lost my boyfriend and other friends. I wanted to talk about how so many wonderful people lost their lives in a matter of minutes. I wanted to talk about how he would never play basketball his senior year, how we never had the chance to go to college together, and how he never had the chance to tell people about who he was. I would give a speech about how gun violence haunts people long after the thoughts and prayers fade away, how I still felt the ghosts of those lost, and how they would remain in my heart forever. Of course, I have never given a speech in public before, so my performance probably would not be as good as it sounded in my head. I'd probably just mutter a few incoherent words. But maybe someday?

Then, as I lost count of how many speeches we'd heard, a familiar face approached the podium. He caught my attention. I knew him. David Williams had been on the debate and forensics team all throughout high school. He was our school's student council vice president although he was only a Junior when the shooting happened, he gave so many interviews in the weeks that followed. Of course, his eloquence meant he received his fair share of asinine criticism. Some blowhard spouted nonsense about how he and others were crisis actors. It felt like the ultimate gaslighting, attacking us for experiencing something horrific by saying we profited from it. Just gross.

David and I were never close. We had a few of the same advanced placement classes, but we rarely talked, except in passing. Yet, at that moment, it felt good to see a familiar face—to see someone who had been through what I had been through. Someone who was still hopeful, at least hopeful enough to keep giving speeches. Did I mention he was on the speech and debate team? His speech was simply magnificent as were all the interviews he gave after the bloodbath in our school.

Thunderous applause erupted after nearly every sentence he shouted. He started by talking about his memories of each of the folks who died in our school and wondered about the many stories cut short in the latest round of shooting. He mentioned Phoebe, who was a first-year at our school when the murderer put several bullets into her:

Phoebe played flute, could always be found with a book, and she liked twirling her large, seemingly unkempt brown hair. I wonder what the title of the book she was reading on that day. I want to finish what Phoebe started and read that last chapter. I wonder if someone like Phoebe died in this last massacre. What books were they reading? What chapters would they never finish? Did they like to twirl their hair, too? Who played the flute? Is their section down a soloist? Did they think about using their flute to fight off the shooter? Did Phoebe?

Then, David started talking about Alex.

Alex was a sophomore when his life ended. Alex enjoyed playing video games. He often wore a superhero shirt or maybe a shirt of a character in his game. He was usually quiet in class but would always try to tell a joke to help someone feel better or lighten the mood. What video game was he playing when the shooting happened? Did he reach the final boss? Was he desperately hoping for a superhero when the bullets started flying? Did he want to try to tell a joke when he was hanging on for life in his hospital bed? What video games lie on the ground unfinished on bedroom floors in the wake of the most recent deaths?

My whole body clenched when I heard David say the next name: Mario.

Mario was a junior. He was already a star athlete. Mario barely missed any of his free throws. But he was also incredibly kind and intelligent. He was probably going to win the state title in basketball the next year. How many unbelievable three-pointers did he still have left in him when the bullets tore through his flesh? Was he thinking about practice and improving his game? Was he thinking about how to be the best team leader he could be? Was he thinking about balancing his academics with earning more accolades? Who is the star athlete at Bay City High? Will they be able to shoot a free throw again? Are they mourning? Are they dead?

My breath was heavy as he spoke. A few sobs escaped as I fought back the tears. I imagined the star athlete killed in the most recent shooting, and I wondered if he had a girlfriend or boyfriend. Did they feel like their life just ended? How would they fill the void left for them? Did they have plans to go to prom? Did they have plans to go to college together? Get married? Each one of our lives is so complex and intricate. How do we move forward when life collapses on itself and is torn apart in such a violent manner?

David continued, sharing his memories of Karla.

Karla was a senior. She loved arguing. She loved it so much that she devoted the last couple of years of her life to debate. She would attend month-long camps in the summer to improve her skills. She was excited to attend college and continue debating. I know she could out-debate any Senator or Representative who votes against common-sense gun safety measures. How many more tournaments could she have won? What classes would she take in college? What debate argument was she brainstorming when it all ended? Did this other school have a debate team? Are they alive to compete once again?

Then, David exclaimed that children are increasingly likely to die from guns, and guns have ended so many lives. He screamed about how every one of them had an unfinished story. Unanswered questions plague us long after the deaths. The what ifs refuse to stop. The dead cannot continue writing their own story, but we can put pen to paper. We can finish the story and make sure it doesn't end here. We have both the opportunity and duty to write a better ending.

The crowd roared in approval as David stepped off the stage. Tears poured down my face. I wished I had gotten to know him better in high school and that I had stayed in touch with him. He knew exactly what I needed to hear.

And with that, the speeches ended, and we started walking. When we marched, I finally noticed how many people had come. For some reason, when we stood on the lawn of the courthouse, the crowd felt small, but maybe I just couldn't see everyone. I marched near the back and am so happy I did. I had a nearly full view of the procession, which went on as far as I could see. At that moment, I felt alive. I felt like we were unstoppable. I felt supported and as if I belonged to a huge community of like-minded people. As you know, I have struggled so much to connect with other people and make bonds. I didn't feel that during the march. I felt tied to all of them, even though I didn't know their names. We felt like one. I cried again, but they were not tears of sadness. For the first time in a long time, I cried because my hope was overwhelming. I cried because I knew we were doing something to prevent further death, and I really believed that.

I tried to find David. I wanted to thank him for his speech and catch up with him. But, after his speech concluded, I didn't even see a hint of him in the enormous crowd. I wanted to reconnect with someone from school, someone who was doing something to change our future and the fates of all students who practiced lockdowns. Someone who was working to end the dreaded phrase: run, hide, fight.

Later, when I got back to my apartment, I hastily typed an email to my Representatives to encourage them to support gun safety measures. Most of them did not need any convincing, but I thought it would be nice to show them that I support their efforts. After I smashed the send button, I found my way to a heated discussion on social media about queer rights. Normally, I would just ignore it. But I chimed in. I felt this indescribable energy to say something, if not for me, then for the other queer folks reading alone. It was like something in my gut would burst if I didn't post something. Maybe I was still high from the march, but my fingers just could not be contained. Or, maybe it was more like my whole body needed to vomit all over these posts to release my overwhelming excitement from the day.

Whatever the reason, I wrote God loves all his creations, even the straight jerks. I prayed I put a little smile on someone's face. It gave me a little chuckle. And I posted a few links to queer-affirming blog posts, movies, and books. I stopped engaging when someone posted an image of a chocolate-covered banana. It took me a minute to figure out what it meant. But, as soon as I did, I decided to "run" and not "fight." People just suck sometimes.

Suddenly, a massive wave of exhaustion smacked me. It was like someone flipped a switch: from functional to "I literally can't anymore," in a matter of seconds. All I wanted to do was nap under my warm comforter. The adrenaline and caffeine from the day must have finally worn off.

What I learned at the protest is perhaps I could become an advocate. I want to start exploring options about how I could study social change in college. Maybe I could be a community organizer or something like that? I know people joke about "paid protesters" and whatnot, but maybe it's something I could do. Could I make a living advocating for a better future for us queer folk and for all of us who have experienced gun violence?

What if I could learn how to deliver a moving speech? What if I could make the difference that finally causes some legislation to pass? What if I could help others feel safer in church, letting them be as God created them? What if I could spend my life crafting a more just world? What if I could plan a march with thousands of people? Right now, that sounds so rewarding and meaningful. I want to investigate further. I want to spend my time ensuring no one else must live through the darkness I have known.

But before I do, I think I still need to face that darkness and despair, and I think it means reliving my time with Mario. Perhaps we can continue talking about him next time?

Session #7

HI AARON,

I'm still working on those breathing exercises you taught me. I learned about them a bit in the mental health facility, but I'm appreciating the reminders. Whenever I think about the shooting at Bay City High School, I pause, close my eyes, and inhale deeply. I remind myself to breathe in for four seconds, hold for four seconds, breathe out for four seconds, and hold again for four seconds. That's been helping calm me, especially when all I want to do is throw something against a wall. I've done the "put cold water on the back of your neck" trick too, but sometimes I'm not around a fountain, so the breathing techniques are so helpful.

I found myself thinking about Mario a lot again this week.

Mario started by asking if he could trust me. His question caught me off guard. Could he trust me?

I muttered a simple, "What?"

Mario repeated, "Can I trust you? The preacher said to find someone you could trust on Sunday. I want to find someone I can trust. I'm hoping that might be you."

He asked the question early in our conversation when we met on Wednesday before youth group. We had barely made any small talk. I didn't mind; small talk annoyed me. I decided that we should go to a local restaurant—The Golden Skillet—because it serves breakfast all day. Mario still didn't know the area very well, and I just told him a lot of folks ate there. There's not much choice in our little town. We have a Bistro, but no high schooler could afford it. There was a chain sandwich shop near the highway, but you couldn't have a discreet conversation there.

It usually felt a bit uncomfortable with all the people crammed into the various rooms at The Golden Skillet. It certainly was not a quiet place. High energy and frantic was more its speed. On the bright side, you could usually have an inconspicuous conversation because of how loud it got.

The Golden Skillet was famous for its cinnamon rolls—these massive plate-sized rolls usually required three sittings to finish. It was Mario's first time eating at The Skillet, so I recommended them to him. I think he fell in love with the first bite; his orgasmic grunt gave him away.

"I think I'm a person others can trust," I word-vomited. After a second, I continued, "At least I want to be."

"I've been struggling a lot the past week," he stated flatly as if satisfied with my rather tentative answer.

"Why?" instinctively fell from my lips.

"A lot of reasons—the move, thinking about starting at a new school, and struggling with my faith," he replied, his voice devoid of emotion. He gazed off into the distance. His smile no longer brightened the room. In less than a second, the conversation already dove into deep and murky waters. Was he struggling with this faith? Why was he telling me?

I struggled to decide what to say next. I never felt comfortable with these conversations. Basically, I have two modes: blurt everything out all at once in a highly inappropriate way or remain quiet and just nod along. The stakes always felt so high, like you needed to know the exact right thing to say when nothing you could say would suffice. Unsure of how to respond, I decided that asking for clarification was my best bet. I proceeded with caution, "And you want to talk about it all with someone? With me?"

"I think so," he said hesitantly.

"Why me?" I blurted out.

He answered, with a chuckle, "Honestly, I don't really have anyone else. This is probably a mistake. I barely know you, but you seemed like an alright person on the way to the event last week."

He paused. His mouth stayed open. A long "ummm" escaped. He nibbled his lip. A quick thought about what it would be like to kiss him popped into my head. I know. I probably shouldn't have been thinking about kissing him, not during a weighty conversation, but that's where my brain went.

Finally, he continued, "I think I noticed you being a little more down after the event than before. Like, a little depressed. I felt the same. I was so excited for it, but it was hard. I wanted it to turn out differently."

My mind flashed back to how I felt when the preacher yelled about the sin of homosexuality. His tortured expression flashed back. I winced at the memory, and my stomach churned. Was he thinking about what I was thinking about? I exhaled and agreed, "Yes, it was hard."

By then, my mind was racing. I could feel the word vomit, ready to spill out again. My natural curiosity and nervousness were a powerful force. I had to say something. I had to know. I continued, "I thought I saw a tear form in your eye at one particular moment of the sermon."

"Oh, you saw that?" he said, biting his lip again.

"Yes, I did. And it made me mad. I was so angry that the sermon would put that painful expression on your face," I exclaimed without filtering my thoughts. My brain was basically on autopilot at this point.

He paused and looked right at me. My heart skipped a beat, *had I gone too far?* I wanted him to stare off into the distance again. I dipped my head. Avoid eye contact at all costs, I told myself. But then he asked, "Were you feeling in pain too?"

I sighed, wondering what I was getting myself into. But I decided that I needed to act brave. I wanted him to know. I looked right at him. "Yes, it was a painful moment for me, too," I said slowly but firmly.

"So, are you questioning your sexuality?" His face appeared startled as the abrupt words escaped his lips. It dawned on me he knew the same nervous energy I was feeling. I imagined the question had wanted to escape for a while. I know it's funny, but it is hard to say the words out loud. At least it was for me. Even when I told my dog the first time, I could barely utter the words— "I am gay." I felt a tightness in my chest and throat. Sorry, it's about to get graphic. But you know the feeling of trying to hold down vomit, like real vomit? That's what it felt like. You want it all to stay inside. But the pressure keeps building and building. Before you know it, it must come out. And, once it is out, you feel better. The pressure is freed. Mario had just released the pressure valve. I could feel it. I would bet all I own that he had almost added a "too" to his question: "Are you questioning your sexuality, too?"

I wanted to throw up, too. I decided to be open and honest with Mario. It felt like I knew him. Maybe I was mistaken, but I wanted to trust him. Looking back on this moment, I realize that it might just have been because I already was developing a crush on him. After seeing him in church, I pondered what kissing him would feel like. And I could barely keep him out of my thoughts ever since. And I wanted to know for sure. I stated the following as clearly as I could: "I've been questioning for a while, but I don't think I have any doubts anymore. I am positive God made me gay."

Mario let out a deep sigh. He squeezed his eyes shut. I saw the slight shift in his face. I was sure tears were attempting to form. Somehow, I knew they were happy tears. After a brief pause, he asked, "How do you know?"

My muscles tensed, and I shifted awkwardly in the booth. I hadn't planned on fielding this question. My heart wished he would just say he was gay, too. I answered the best I could, "I just find guys attractive. Last year, especially, I only felt 'turned on' or whatever when I looked at a guy. I prayed for it. Nothing changed. I practically begged God to change me, to cure me, or whatever. But, when I asked God to change me, the answer was 'no'."

"You are so brave about it, letting other people know. I would be so scared to tell someone," he replied.

"Well, you're the first person I've told," I replied. "I mean, I told my dog before, and he's been wonderful—very supportive and a great listener."

Mario chuckled as I continued, "But I thought I could tell you. I guess I don't know why, but I think it's because, even though we just met, we know a lot about each other. During the sermon, I saw the pain that I often feel on your face. That's the only way I know how to explain it."

We sat in silence for a moment. Had I pushed too far, too quickly? The silence became more and more awkward, at least for me. I hate silence. But I also have never been confident in my ability to keep a conversation going. Finally, he continued, "Yes, I imagine we have had many similar experiences. And you are also the first person I've talked to about this."

"So, you have been thinking about your sexuality too?" I asked.

"Yeah, I have," he stated. "But I am not as confident as you are that God wants me to be like this. Find guys so attractive, you know."

"But you never choose to have those feelings. God just made you that way," I exclaimed. The words slipped out so easily. I made a little mental note to myself: next time

I am feeling uncertain about who I am, just remember how simple these words were to say.

Finally, his smile had returned to his face. "I love how confident you are," he said. "I desperately want to be that confident."

"Stick with me, and I will show you that God loves you exactly as you are," I said. "That's a promise." My mouth said those words, but it felt awkward being called confident. Confidence is among the last words I would ever use to describe me. I frankly surprised myself. I didn't think I would ever be so forward. Maybe my unconscious just knew I needed to talk to someone about all of this; I needed to let someone in.

"Well, then you have to pinky swear!" He laughed.

I reached over, offering my pinky finger to him, and he did the same. Our fingers locked. My heart skipped a beat as a little jolt of electricity worked its way up my arm.

Afterward, we paid and headed off to youth group. It was the last youth group before the school year started. Miraculously, I would be starting my freshman year with someone who knew. Mario and I knew each other. We saw each other. I already felt so close to him.

For the first time in a long time, I felt warm and could barely contain myself. I could not wait for what adventures awaited Mario and me.

Session #8

A AARON,

Is it normal to feel like your mental health is regressing? I felt like we had made some progress, but now it's like I am back to square one.

You said being honest is necessary for healing. They also told me transparency is key in the mental health facility, especially if your meds were causing constipation. Well, I am struggling. I am so frustrated by all the politicians who use queer rights to stir up their base. It's shameful. What is more shameful is how well it works. It is hard for me to avoid thinking about how much better my life might have been if people had talked openly about sexuality in school or if I had the chance to read a book with a gay character. Why is something as simple as wanting some recognition for whom you are so controversial? We read so many books and articles about straight folks, and they included plenty of sexual innuendo. Just think of all the sex jokes in Romeo and Juliet!

In one class, we read a story about how some short guy was a brave hero for asking a tall girl out on a date. A hero? Really? Queers are heroes when they risk everything to tell others about who they are. We are heroes who must risk violence simply for daring to love who we love. A short guy asking out a tall girl is not heroic. It is normal. Mundane.

And I know I shouldn't focus too much on these hateful pieces of legislation because I don't have much control. But I cannot help it. I try to tell myself the serenity prayer.

God, grant me the serenity to accept the things I cannot change,

the courage to change the things I can,

and the wisdom to know the difference.

I try to accept the things I cannot change, but I just can't. It feels immoral to look away. People might get hurt. People do get hurt, and I just feel like I must do something to help. I recently read that the mere introduction of an anti-queer piece of legislation causes spikes in calls to mental health crisis lines. I contact my representatives, but it feels like such a waste of time. Either they already support queer rights, or they oppose them, and my email changes nothing. They just put us on some stupid mailing list.

That's why I researched classes on how to advocate for others and myself. When I watch other students advocating against gun violence or drag queens demanding the respect they deserve, I know it's what *I* want to do. I found one class called public advocacy—I can take it next semester. I do not know where this will take me, but I do know I want to try to better the world. What's the worst that could happen?

I want a world where two young gay boys can be open about their relationship. Mario and I were denied the right.

I remember the first day of sophomore year like it was yesterday. Ever since we talked about our sexualities, my heart skipped a beat when I thought about what I to say when I saw him next. Frankly, I surprised myself. When I talked with him, I felt more confident about myself. I know God made me gay, and it was beautiful. Around him, I felt warm, happy, and understood.

Perhaps I let my mental image of a brighter future with him get away from me. The first day of freshman year sucked. Mario found me before school started. I was meandering around the band room when he approached and muttered the flat, quiet words, "Hey, can we talk?"

"Yeah, sure," I whispered.

We walked out of earshot. As soon as we did, I asked, "Hey, what's up?"

"Well, I thought we should talk a little bit about what we discussed last Wednesday," he said.

"About our sexualities?" The words left my lips without a second of thought.

"Yes, I just thought we should make sure we are on the same page about not talking about it to anyone," He continued.

"Yeah, I guess it's for the best. I don't want to be the talk of the school," I responded. I knew he would not want to talk about it. Heck, I probably did not want to tell anyone, either. Being out would have caused so much hardship. It was hard to go a day without hearing a slur or gay joke. Too many of the teachers would just sit there and not do anything when it happened. Yet, a small part of me still hurts because I wanted to date. I wanted people to know being gay is a beautiful thing. I wanted to work up the courage to ask Mario to go to a dance with me, but I also knew it would probably never happen.

"Especially while I am still figuring everything out. And, I just have a feeling that people here will not be very supportive or accepting," he added.

"Exactly, but we can still talk about it, right? I really enjoyed talking with you last week," I uttered.

"Yes, of course!" he answered, "Heck, I almost want to skip school just to chat with you."

"Really?" I asked.

"I mean, maybe not. My parents would kill me if I let my grades slip," he said. "But I would definitely enjoy talking with you more than going to class."

"Me too!" I replied. Again, I instantly wondered if I was acting too excited. Fortunately, I didn't have too much time to think about it.

The bell rang a moment later, and we headed off to class.

I struggled to pay attention all day long. Whenever I came close to regaining my focus, my mind looped back to him and our conversation. A part of me knew he was right; we shouldn't talk about our sexuality with people at school. Another part of me thought it was wrong; we shouldn't have to hide who we are. Of course, if the world weren't so homophobic, we wouldn't have to deal with any of this.

Throughout the year and the rest of our time in high school, people frequently asked us if we were dating anyone. Well, people asked Mario about his relationships. I hardly ever got the question. Let's be honest, Mario was stunning. I never felt as attractive as him; I know he would stop me from putting myself down if he heard me saying this. But it's just the truth. He was a ten, and I often felt generous giving myself a seven.

Every time Mario fielded one of those questions, it stung a little; especially when we did start dating. He pretended he wanted to focus on sports and improving his game. When I was asked, I told people my grades mattered the most to me. I wasn't looking for a distraction. For all they knew, I was being a good little Christian boy. I was saving it for marriage. At least, that's the image I desperately wanted to cultivate for myself. But, if we had come out, we would not have had to field those questions. We would not have to lie. Worse, lying became so familiar to us. It became second nature. After you lie so many times, a part of it starts to feel like the truth. Can you really know who you are if you continue to lie about it?

I am so happy for the young queer teenagers who are coming out now. I want a world where two gay freshmen are just as comfortable letting people know about their relationship as two straight freshmen. And I want a world where those two gay love birds seem just as cute to everyone else. It's one of the many reasons I want to become an advocate or something similar. I want to fight for a better world for all the Marios out there who are too scared to let anyone know.

Session #9

H EY AARON,

It was a few weeks into our freshman year of high school. We enjoyed youth group, with the colossal exception of the trip to Big Rapids. But I look back on another night with pain and sadness. The night left deep wounds. I don't think I will ever fully recover, and I guess that's a recurring theme for me. I wonder if I will ever heal or even if I should. I hope my pain is useful to others someday. I often wonder if God is testing me like he tested Job. In the Book of Job, God basically gambles with the Devil about Job's devotion. God gave the Devil reign over Job. Job lost everything—his livestock, children, and his health. It is hard not to imagine and wonder what I am about to lose next. Why does God test us like this? It seems harsh, and it is hard not to feel angry and resentful.

That night, the discussion topic for the youth group focused on love and how to show God's love toward others. People said some of the usual things you would expect to hear. They would quote, maybe inaccurately, the passage about love not being about boasting and about love being patient and kind. Another person talked about how love is about giving yourself for others—the way Jesus did for us when he died on the cross. Oddly, the conversation quickly shifted to who was capable of loving. I imagine you know where this is going—the topic of same-sex marriages. Were gay people really in love, or was it just sinful lust? Like a broken record, folks blurted the usually hateful statements about queer people: "It is not how God wanted us to love," "it is sinful," and "it just doesn't work biologically."

I don't think I felt angry—just sad. Maybe empty? What if they knew about me? What if they knew about Mario? Would they still believe these awful clichés? After hearing several of these comments, I foolishly asked, "I wonder, though, if we are supposed to love gay people. If all people are made in God's image, aren't they, as well?"

"Are rapists and pedophiles made in God's image?" One of the leaders immediately responded. He caught me off guard, to say the least. I didn't say anything for the rest of the discussion. Maybe I was in shock. I tried to look over at Mario, but he was looking at the leader who asked the question.

Back then, I had no idea what to say or do. Now, I know I have a better response. Homophobia no longer surprises me in the way it used to. Now, I would say queer people consent to their relationships. Love exists in those relationships where it doesn't in moments of sexual violence. Sexual violence is sinful lust. I could also suggest that being gay is not a choice; God made me a gay man. The sin is violence; the sin is not being in love with another man. I guess I could have said a lot of things. Yet, at the time, I froze; I could not muster a single word.

That loaded question, which assumes being gay is on the same level as committing sexual assault, wounded us. It was the stab in the back we didn't see coming. We witnessed once again what people really thought about us and how they would treat us if they knew.

Later that night, Mario called me, "Hey! How are you?"

"Fine, I guess," I responded.

"How are you feeling about youth group?" he asked.

"I don't really know. Sad, mostly, I think. It just hurts. My soul hurts," I replied.

"Yeah, I know what you mean. I was a bit angry at first. We were supposed to be talking about love, and yet the discussion was filled with so much hate," Mario exclaimed.

"Exactly!" I responded. "We were discussing how to show God's love, and all I could feel was hate and anger. It's the exact opposite of love is patient, love is kind, love is not rude, love is not quick to anger."

Mario chuckled, "Yeah, you would think they could catch the irony."

He laughed again and sighed. After a pause, he continued, "So, I think I am realizing I need something other than our youth group to explore my relationship with God and my sexuality."

"Yeah? What do you have in mind?" I asked.

"Well, I did a little bit of research, and I found these videos, like documentaries, which focus on gay Christians and their families. It might give us a role model or something. Someone to explain why we are feeling attracted to other men." He spoke hesitantly at first but then seemed to become more confident as he continued. He added, "I found the copies at the library in Big Rapids and checked them out. Do you want to watch them with me?"

I responded without thinking, "Yes! I would love to."

Anyway, ever since Mario questioned how helpful our youth group was for us, I have consistently found it difficult to find God in church. I feel God in strange places—places that most Christians would characterize as sinful or at a protest.

Last week, I found God watching drag queens perform. I'm proud of myself for attending our university's fourth annual show. Ever since I lost Mario, I struggle to go to queer spaces or events without him. It is bittersweet. Whenever I go, I feel him. It's like he is watching me from above. I feel his warmth. I feel his infectious energy. I feel his soft, loving embrace. At first, it always puts a little smile on my face. But then I remember he's gone from me; I can't ask him how he's feeling. I cannot hold his hand. He cannot embrace me and tell me everything will be alright. I will never see his smile coming at me out of the rest of the crowd. I felt confident with him, and I have struggled to act bravely since.

At the drag show, I felt a warmth—an internal glow—once again. As I walked into the room that's normally a place to get lunch, the smile sneaked onto my face. I took a deep breath. One queen had started performing before I arrived. The crowd yelled gleefully. A tear of joy started forming as I watched all these diverse people coming together as one—as a community of people who loved and supported queer folks. Everyone seemed so happy. It was beautiful. I wondered how anyone could find this display of love and happiness anything other than a miracle. That's how it was for me. Strangely, in these moments, I feel

God with me. I feel seen and understood by someone who is not physically present but is with me, in my soul.

I glanced up at the ceiling, pausing a moment to feel the warmth of Mario's embrace. I looked back to the stage as the queen jumped up and did the splits. The crowd, as they say, went wild. My smile grew wider as I took a step forward and lived this miracle.

I haven't always felt so good. In fact, I still recall the time I barely existed.

Session #10

HEY AARON,

Immediately after the shooting, my life essentially became a drunken haze. I wasn't drinking, but I desperately wanted to. At least, I thought I wanted to. I've never tasted any kind of alcohol. It's a miracle I didn't during that time. I wanted it so badly.

I felt numb, like something had just sucked all the happiness and joy out of the world. I tried not to think about Mario and the others who didn't make it, but their memories would come flooding back to me. When they did, I couldn't help the following waves of salty tears. One day, I was shopping for a new pair of shoes. A pair reminded me of Mario's favorite sneakers; I shook with cold, and the nausea was rising; I couldn't control myself. I sprinted out of the store and went home, exhausted.

All I wanted to do was sleep. For weeks. I only left my bed when the hunger became so unbearable that my stomach overpowered my brain. I slept, and slept, and slept. I could scarcely keep my eyes open. Whenever I slept, I woke up even more tired. It became easier and easier just to go back to sleep.

It was strange. At first, I thought I would never be able to sleep again. Would the nightmares about the shooting come? Would Mario's bloody face torture me over and over and over again? Would I hear the screams? But my dreams just turned off, and fortunately, I didn't dream at all.

I didn't have nightmares until later. For a few weeks, I found so much peace by simply sleeping. It was like I didn't exist. I didn't have to feel anything. I didn't have to think about anything. No one expected anything from me, which almost got me in a lot of trouble with school.

When my depression was at its worst, I refused to leave my bed. I could not make myself get up. Energy drained from my body. Days went by without me realizing it. I barely go to school. I only go when my parents chase me out of bed. And, even when I do go, I normally dip at lunchtime to head home and take a nap. Sometimes, I make it back for my last period of the day. Sometimes, I wake up in the middle of the night, my stomach growling for something to eat. Sometimes, I would satisfy my craving. Sometimes, I don't. I have lost close to fifteen pounds in the months following the shooting.

By the time I got back in a rhythm, I barely recognized school, and I really struggled to follow what was happening in my classes. Fortunately, summer break was around the corner, and I don't think anyone wanted to be at school. My over-enthusiastic band teacher had become lethargic, and he looked like he was on the verge of collapsing while conducting. My Spanish teacher stopped requiring us to speak in Spanish. My math teacher let us watch movies involving math, like *Stand and Deliver*. I don't think my teachers wanted to teach; I think they wanted to mourn along with the rest of us. They couldn't blame me for wanting to stay wrapped in my warm blankets all day, could they? Heck, I bet a few of them didn't want to step back into school anymore. We were all traumatized, and we all just wanted summer. We wanted it so bad.

Sadly, I barely remember Mario's funeral. I know I went; I still have the little bookmark they handed out. The bookmark itself was amusingly stereotypical. It showed two clouds splitting apart with light shining through them. One simple dove looked like it was flying into the light: a simple dove flying toward heaven. Below the scene, a passage from Matthew was written in a small font: "Come to me, all you who are weary and burdened, and I will give you rest."

I read and re-read the passage repeatedly, trying my best to convince myself that Mario was in a better place. He no longer had to feel the stinging pain of homophobia and discrimination. He no longer had to worry about how he would come out to his parents. He no longer had to wonder if he would ruin his basketball career by letting people know he liked boys. He would no longer have to contend with being, as he would say, a Hispanic in a racist world. He no longer needed to listen to fellow Christians demean and malign him. He finally found rest from this harsh world.

I must admit. I envied him. I wanted to rest, too. Maybe that's why I just slept and slept and slept some more. I wanted to wake up one day somewhere where I did not have to think about whether I was a sinner. I wanted to wake up one day and forget all about the painful homophobic jokes or slurs I heard daily. I wanted to wake up one day and know the gender of the person I loved didn't matter. I wanted to wake up one day and witness other Christians loudly proclaim they love and affirm queer folks. I wanted to wake up one day and never have to worry about feeling pain and being so exhausted I could barely move. I wanted to wake up one day and realize this was all a terrible dream.

I never woke up on any of those days. Others made sure the world kept spinning. Slowly, parents and students came together to figure out how to move forward without forgetting what we had lost. Parents and students gave interviews to the local, state, and even national news. All the big news channels ran short special reports about us and how the city was trying to move forward and rebuild.

The Parent-Teachers Association created a scholarship in honor of the fifteen who died; it became an essay contest. The news of the scholarship went national, and I am convinced they received an obscene number of donations. The scholarship winner would be the student who best crafted an argument about how society could improve school safety and address gun violence. Of course, the first wave of scholarships all went to survivors of the shooting, so it did not really feel like a contest. I never wrote anything for it. I didn't want to think about gun violence. I know others did. I knew they wanted to start organizations to help others in a similar situation. I knew they wanted to persuade as many lawmakers as they could to pass a law. And I was happy for them. I'm glad some folks could talk about it and use their voice. But I just could not bring myself to do that at first. I didn't even mention the shooting in any of my college applications.

The school ended up putting up a plaque honoring everyone who died. It said something like, "We will always remember those we lost," and it listed all the names in small font at the bottom. Whenever I walked past it, I really wished it mentioned they died in a school shooting. Something about how vague the plaque was really irked me. I didn't want to sanitize the past. I wanted people to remember the horror and carnage the way I always did. I wanted them to remember the blood stains and the screaming. I didn't want anyone to move on.

Frankly, I appreciate all the efforts to remember the fifteen, but it never feels like it was enough. It feels superficial like we were patting ourselves on the back for doing something. But what we did would never be enough.

Session #11

H ᴇʏ Aᴀʀᴏɴ,

This week, I've thought a lot about how Mario and I explored our identities together, especially when we watched queer-themed movies.

Mario had the popcorn ready when I arrived at his house that Saturday. Fortunately for us, his parents had to work all day. We would be alone. We would be free to speak openly and honestly with each other.

"We could make a pizza if you want," Mario started as I took a handful of popcorn.

"I think this is good for now. I've been looking forward to this movie since you mentioned it!" I exclaimed.

We sat down together on his couch. It was remarkably comfy. I remember being a little nervous about where to sit. I didn't want to sit too close, to make it uncomfortable, and to make it seem like a date because it wasn't. Or was it? Anyway, I didn't want to sit too far away either because that was awkward, too.

Plus, it would be more difficult to talk. I guess it was a little cringy for Mario to watch as I sat down and then hopped a little bit further away, and then hopped back closer to him. The popcorn sat between us, and, no, we never had a "Lady and the Tramp" moment where our hands touched, and we felt a spark. The night was void of any spark.

I confess I wanted the spark to happen. I was infatuated with him since our first "breakfast" together at The Golden Skillet. He exuded kindness, love, and intelligence. It also helped that God sculpted him to perfection.

"Are you ready for this?" he asked as he grabbed the remote to press play.

"I think so! I'm nervous but also excited, you know?" I answered.

"I know what you mean. I hope this helps me understand a bit more about, well, everything," He continued as the opening music started playing.

We stayed mostly quiet throughout the film, except for munching on the popcorn. The documentary packed a punch, and I felt tears forming in my eyes throughout the whole film. It followed four families who were devout Christians but then had a family member come out as queer. One story broke my heart. It was a mother discussing how her son had died by suicide and how she was devoting the rest of her life to fighting against discrimination in the church. I wondered if my mother would do the same. I wanted to say she would, but uncertainty overwhelmed me when I thought about it.

Another story followed a pastor whose daughter came out as lesbian. The pastor and his wife both struggled with accepting their daughter. They still called being queer as a sin. They had put their limited views about God's word ahead of their daughter. Thank God Mario had tissues! Water streamed down our cheeks.

But I also cried tears of joy and hope as we watched the other stories.

One family rallied to support their gay son and argue against those in their church who held homophobic beliefs. They became advocates. They challenged organizations who promoted hateful beliefs about queer people. The mother and son were arrested together, praying and protesting. Beautiful, I thought. The final story followed a father who became politically engaged as well. He fought for marriage equality both within and outside of the church. He'd previously struggled to understand his son's sexuality, but he changed his mind when he saw the love between his son and his son's boyfriend, now husband. He said it was the same love he had felt for his wife, who recently passed away. He delivered speeches at his City Council urging more support for queer people. He wrote letters to political leaders. He published opinion pieces in his local newspaper. The documentary showed me the wide range of possibilities in my future. It scared and inspired me in equal measure.

Yet, one thing remained consistent throughout the film. Each queer individual stayed adamant in their identity as a queer Christian. They spoke with such confidence. They knew God loved them. They knew they would find love in this world. They knew they were queer. I think I fell a bit in love with their certainty. I told myself that one day, I would have more confidence in myself. Like them, I would know God's love despite those who told me I couldn't find it if I was gay.

As the end credits started, I turned to Mario. Tears still rolled down his face. Tentatively, I asked, "So, what did you think?"

"It was beautiful," he responded, still staring at the television. "Just wow."

"I loved the confidence they had as they talked about being a queer Christian. I want to be that brave someday," I stated.

"Yeah, I know what you mean. They knew who they were, and they were not afraid to share it with others, even if it meant cutting folks out of their lives who didn't support them," Mario uttered slowly and a bit more somberly. He continued, "I don't know if I am strong enough to do that. I don't want to lose my relationship with my family. I worry my parents might react similarly to the pastor."

"I wonder how mine would react. I would love to say they would be supportive and get rainbow flags or whatever. But I don't think they would. They've sat through plenty of sermons about homosexuality being a sin," I said, my voice shaky.

"At least we will have each other," he said.

"I know . . ." I replied. "I feel a lot less lonely now."

"Right?" He said, "The loneliness is the hard part, I think. Never knowing who you can talk to."

"Being afraid at every turn," I agreed. "And you just pray that someone will come along and affirm you."

He continued, "Well then, I guess it is important to tell you I am so thankful you're in my life, and I have someone to talk to about all this stuff."

"I'm thankful about it, too," I replied. "I'm glad you came to our youth group."

"Maybe I could have waited a few weeks to start." He chuckled.

I instantly recalled the horrid field trip we went on. I smiled and rolled my eyes. He continued, "Want to watch the next movie?"

"Sure!"

If I wasn't so intrigued by the subject matter, I would have found the second film rather dull and boring. It was less emotional and more logical than the first documentary. The narrator went through every biblical passage which seemingly condemned same-sex relationships. Professors of theology and pastors, and queer Christians read these so-called texts of terror. It was the first time I had heard any part of the Bible called a terror, but it clicked with me. Apparently, a feminist theologian coined the term to describe the passages that have been, and could be, used to justify sexism. I knew people used parts of scripture to do harm, based on sexuality, race, religion, sex, and so much more. That harm terrorized people like me and Mario. I think people got so used to the terror that they couldn't feel anything other than shame, anger, and fear of scripture.

Those advocating for a queer-inclusive understanding of scripture kept emphasizing the importance of context. The historical context helped them have a better understanding of what God was communicating and commanding. Many of them mentioned that the passages in Leviticus likely referred to nonconsensual or coerced sexual activity, like temple prostitution or sexual violence. One of the commentators explained the story of Sodom and Gomorrah, revealing it was about violence and hospitality towards the stranger, not loving same-sex relationships and that many Christians failed to welcome the queer strangers in their midst. The distinction between consensual and non-consensual sex made sense to me as we would condemn non-consensual sex in any relationship, or at least I hoped we would.

One queer Christian pastor said she read certain parts of scripture through a queer lens. I understood her to mean she assumed scripture affirmed queer folks, so we saw more queerness in scripture than the average person.. For her, the Bible affirmed queer and loving relationships. She mentioned the story of David and Jonathan in 1 Samuel. The same David who slayed the giant Goliath would later meet Jonathan, the son of the King. And this pastor suggested that giant-slaying David loved Jonathan.

Before she finished her thought, Mario paused the movie, jumped up, and ran to grab his family's Bible. I think I heard him mutter something like, "Be right back," but I wasn't certain.

A second later, he returned breathing more heavily than before. He exclaimed, "Listen to this, Jason. 1 Samuel 18, 'After David had finished talking with Saul, Jonathan became one in spirit with David, and he loved him as himself. From that day, Saul kept David with him and did not let him return home to his family. And Jonathan made a covenant with David because he loved him as himself. Jonathan took off the robe he was wearing and gave it to David, along with his tunic, and even his sword, his bow and his belt.' I never realized this was in scripture before!"

"I thought most people just said they had a really good friendship," I murmured, a little confused at the passage and a bit startled by Mario's sudden excitement about it. I thought Mario might start jumping up and down on the couch cushions.

"I mean, he basically stripped in front of him. Sounds pretty gay to me," Mario replied, smirking. "Maybe bi?"

"Maybe?" I continued with some hesitation. Someone might call my trepidation internalized homophobia, but it really did puzzle me that a gay couple could be represented in scripture.

"I wonder if people just assumed it was a good friendship because the thought that they might be more never crossed their minds," Mario continued.

"They assume scripture condemns gay relationships, so they read any possible queer relationship as not gay?" I meant it as a statement, but it sounded more like a question when I uttered it.

"Exactly," Mario replied. "What if they loved each other? Wouldn't that be amazing?"

I was about to say yes, but my cell phone vibrated. They must be waiting outside, I thought. Of course, my parents would call right when I wanted the moment to last longer—when all I wanted to do was keep talking with him.

"Can we chat about this some other time?" Mario asked.

"Yes, I would love that," I replied.

"Me too," he stated. "But quick before you leave. I need to tell you something."

"Yeah?" I asked.

"I haven't said it out loud yet, but yeah, I'm … gay." He replied with a sigh of relief.

"Thanks for letting me know," I said.

Session #12

DEAR AARON,

I don't recall exactly, but I think it was like three weeks after we watched the documentaries. Mario and I decided to meet up again to talk about sexuality and religion. Mario had been texting me non-stop about the whole David and Jonathan might be a gay couple thing. It was mostly just little statements like "they were basically making out" or "dude, he loved him more than he loved women." I felt his eagerness and excitement pouring through the screen with each text.

It didn't help that he continued researching the possibility of queer folks being in the Bible. Apparently, he found another book at the library written by the woman in the documentary. It was an awakening for him.

The texts quickly came, one after another after another.

"Did you know that the words 'until death do us part' were spoken between two women?"

"What if we thought about Jesus as being an asexual individual?"

"Just a reminder, he literally stripped in front of him."

The texts kept coming, and I had no clue what he was talking about for a few of them.

"Ruth and Naomi. The great lesbians of scripture."

"We really need to talk about the passages about eunuchs."

"For there are eunuchs who were born that way, and there are eunuchs who were made eunuchs by others—and there are those who choose to live like eunuchs for the sake of the kingdom of heaven."

"Maybe that's about being intersex or asexual?"

"I just read about those terms last week."

"David loved Jonathan. Think we could get that on a bumper sticker?"

"Literally stripped, Jason. Not straight guy behavior!"

The more he texted, the more I couldn't help smiling and laughing. His excitement was as contagious as always. His infectious joy radiated, and you could feel how happy he was we could find ourselves in scripture, if only we had the courage to put on our queer lenses.

When we finally got to meet in person again, he had far too many books. Maybe five or six? Thankfully, we had just started winter break. Otherwise, I would've worried he might fall behind in all his classes. He still had basketball practice. At least, I thought he did. Still, it was impressive how much he'd been reading. I'd started researching a bit, but Mario was devouring every word he could.

It was another Saturday, and his parents were at work again. The smell of popcorn lingered in the air. As we walked into the living room, the books were stacked next to the couch. Mario stated, "Well, I checked out a few movies about gay... stuff we could watch. Or we could chat about the books I've been reading. I'm just excited to get to talk about all of this with you again."

"Huh? Okay, we got plenty to choose from, it looks like," I said as my eyes roved over the stack of four or five movies on the wooden end table.

"Yeah, I guess we do. I might have gone a little overboard when I was at the library. But how could I say no to free things? And, I really did not want to have to keep making trips to Big Rapids' library," he laughed.

"True," I responded. "Well, what do you want to do?"

"Well, I sort of want to watch one of the movies. A few of them are like romance movies but also deal with religion," he replied.

"Sounds good to me," I answered.

Mario grabbed one of the DVDs and rushed over to get everything set up.

I grabbed my bowl of popcorn, shoved a handful in my mouth, and sat in the same spot I had last time. And, of course, I got some popcorn on my shirt. Quickly brushing it all off, I asked Mario, "What is this one about?"

"It's like a romance between this guy who was raised in a really conservative Christian household and a guy who is like the exact opposite," Mario answered as he finished setting up.

The "exact opposite" was right. In the opening scene, the guy was dancing as a go-go boy at a gay club. He wore what I could only describe as a thong. You could see almost everything: his glistening abs, his voluptuous butt cheeks, and how well-endowed he was.

"Damn, he is attractive," Mario exclaimed instantly.

"Right?!" I answered, finally free to express my desires with someone I had felt comfortable with. More than that, Mario made me feel safe, safe to be who I am.

The movie had everything: sex scenes, an awkward first interaction where one guy tripped over the other, deep conversations about faith and sexuality, and concern for each other mentally and spiritually. The go-go dancer worried about the mental health of his soon-to-be boyfriend, and the conservatively raised guy expressed concern about the other's spiritual well-being, at least at first. Of course, they upset each other when they first shared their feelings and flippantly rejected each other's remarks. But eventually they talked through everything, started understanding each other, and hooked up. And hooked up again. And again. One might say they fell in love.

When it ended, I looked over at Mario. A feeling of safety and warmth lingered with me, and all I could do was smile.

He was the first to talk: "I really never wanted it to end."

"It was beautiful," I agreed. "What was your favorite part?"

"I'm glad they found each other," Mario continued. Then, looking over at me, "And I'm glad I found you."

If I was not mistaken, he was on the verge of choking up a bit, and I thought I heard a little crack as he spoke. It instantly changed how I was processing the situation; the film really moved Mario. His voice sounded hopeful, but he also sounded a bit nervous. He had revealed how much he cared about me and our relationship.

I responded in kind, "I am so glad I have you too."

Sunday rolled around, and we found ourselves chatting with each other over lemonade and cookies like normal.

"Yesterday was awesome, but I really need to practice for tryouts," Mario said.

"Tryouts?" I asked.

"Yeah, basketball tryouts are this week," Mario answered.

"Already?" I exclaimed.

"Yeah, they really snuck up on me," Mario said.

"Well, it is a good thing you haven't stopped practicing," I replied.

"Yeah, and I have been running a lot to stay in shape," Mario said.

I paused for a second, not really wanting to say what I thought of his body out loud in church.

"Did you think about doing cross-country?" I asked.

"I don't think we moved in time," he replied. "But I'm going to next year."

"Cool," I said. "Need some company while you practice today?"

"Sure," he said. "I'm not sure how fun it will be watching me, though."

"I'm sure I'll manage," I said, smirking inside.

After letting our parents know, Mario and I walked to a nearby playground. I didn't know much about basketball, but he did make more of the shots than he missed. That had to be a good sign, right?

Tryouts lasted until the day of youth group. We decided we'd go from school to church. I studied and worked on homework in the library. I read and re-read some of my notes until I was getting bored. I thought about him and how tryouts were going. Under the desk, my legs were shaking, and my heartbeat faster than normal. I guess it was nerves.

The library closed before tryouts finished, so I wandered over to his car and waited. I kicked some dirt around and leaned on the hood.

Eventually, he saw me and yelled, "I did it! I made varsity!"

He sprinted toward me, and I exclaimed, "Congratulations! That's awesome!"

A moment later, he was right in front of me. Suddenly, his arms opened, and he came in for a hug. Startled, I froze. His arms were just sort of squishing mine. He had taken a shower, so he was still a bit wet. He smelled a little woodsy. *Interesting...deodorant? Cologne?* He smelt so good after showering. I could hear the smile in his voice. "I'm so happy. The coach said I was impressive during the tryouts."

"I'm so happy for you," I said as he slowly released his grip on me.

"Promise me you'll come to every game this season?" he asked as his hands slid down my forearm, moving slowly towards my hands. A buzz of magnetic energy came out of nowhere, and I wanted nothing more than to hold his hand.

"Of course, I'll be there," I said softly but firmly. A warm fuzzy feeling came over me, my heart reaching for his.

Then, a bunch of cars started honking in the distance. We both jumped apart in shock. The magnetism vanished as if it had never existed.

"Well, we should probably start heading toward to youth group," he stated and reached for his car door.

Session #13

DEAR AARON,

The last few weeks of the fall semester went by in a blur. Mario and I had so much to do. Between Mario's work, his basketball practice, and our homework, we only really saw each other on youth group days.

We not-very-patiently waited for winter break. Mario saw an advertisement for a new queer coming-of-age movie coming to theaters on December 30. The preview looked like the exact type of movie that we wanted to see together. A cute gay high school student had to decide if he wanted to come out as he pursued his goal of having a boyfriend before the end of college. The film marked the first time we'd ever heard of any mainstream films about young gay folks. We instantly made plans to go to a theater in Big Rapids under the cover of wanting to check out some post-Christmas deals.

Thankfully, winter break arrived before we knew it. The chilly air forced us to wear jackets, which put Mario in the mood for a peppermint mocha. We stopped and grabbed two on the way to Big Rapids. We sipped the holiday deliciousness.

Mario started the conversation, "How pumped are you for this?"

"Incredibly!" I answered. "It can't come soon enough."

"I'm probably going to get irked by the previews at the beginning," Mario exclaimed.

"I know, right? Just show us the gay stuff already!" I responded.

Mario paused briefly and I felt the tone of the conversation shifting. He said, "Six months ago, I would have never imagined I would be out to someone and going to a queer movie."

"I know. Me neither," I replied.

"I'm glad I didn't lose hope, but I really thought I would. You know, with the move and thinking about being gay and that awful sermon on my first day of youth group," Mario continued. "I really thought I would give up."

It was hard for me to believe. Mario had always been a beacon of light for me. Optimistic, devoted, and dedicated were some of his defining characteristics. It reminded me of a quote; I can't remember it in full, but it's something about how the most joyful and caring people are those who have experienced the most pain.

"You've a rough go of it," I replied, not exactly sure what I should say.

"The bright spot was meeting you," he said.

Blood and heat flushed my face, and my heart soared. I replied, "I'm so happy I met you too."

Eventually, we arrived at the theater. Mario had already bought the tickets online, so I told him I'd get the popcorn. Thankfully, Mario didn't like butter on his popcorn—just like me. I hate the sensation of sticky hands all movie long.

We found our seats in the back of the theater. When the previews started, Mario nudged me with his elbow. Even without looking at him, I could sense the smirk on his face. I nudged him back, spilling a bit of the popcorn. Mario laughed and whispered, "Careful."

"You started it," I replied with a little laugh, too.

He reached in, grabbed a handful of popcorn, and smashed it into his face. Crumbs fell onto his shirt—his grin now mischievous. I just smiled and shook my head.

The film started, and my heart pounded with excitement. A rush of warmth came over me, and I smiled. I was sitting next to another gay guy in a movie theater about to watch a gay movie... I never wanted it to end. I wanted the world to stop turning. I wanted time to freeze. I wanted to sit here next to Mario forever in our bubble of joy and happiness.

During the first half of the movie, the main character struggled with his sexuality. Mario and I struggled with our timing and coordination. Several times, our hands awkwardly met in the popcorn tub. We should have bought two. Each time, a nervous jolt of energy rushed its way up from my hand, through my arm, and into my brain. Our hands immediately retreated to our sides, and we whispered, "Sorry."

As the film progressed, I could not help falling in love with the main character. He was exactly like me. He had religious parents, and he worried whether they would leave him if they ever knew. He prayed and prayed for God to change him. He wanted to be normal. He wanted to be straight. It may sound strange at first, but a scene about halfway through the movie brought tears to my eyes. He had a cute little dog named Porky. The little pug sat there and gave him kiss after kiss as he came out to this dog, "Porky, I wanted to tell you something about myself... I'm gay...and I wanted to let you know."

I felt the tang of salty water starting to trickle its way down my face, but I picked up on a strange energy.

Then, I really felt it. A little pressure on my hand. It was Mario's hand, reaching out for my own. It was magnetic, like our hearts were reaching for each other.

I turned my hand over and slowly clasped my hand around his.

I squeezed his hand a little more. His hand warmed mine, and the warmth flooded up my arm and to my face. I knew he was smiling without having to look, and I felt like his smile had appeared on my face.

I forced myself to stay in the moment. My mind wanted to race. I wanted to think about what this could all mean. I wanted to ask if this meant we were boyfriends. I wanted to know if he anticipated us going further. But I did not let my mind take over. I just watched the fireworks and held onto his hand. Slowly, another tear emerged in the corner of my eye. If I had felt any happier, I might have burst.

On the way home, we listened to music and laughed. All the cares and concerns in my life didn't matter. I was with him. And he was smiling. I was smiling. Nothing else mattered, with one exception. I wondered what the handholding meant. Neither of us mentioned it. Neither of us wanted to ruin the magical moment.

The credits rolled, and we sat there together a moment longer. Mario's hand set mine loose. He whispered, "Just amazing."

"Our first gay-themed movie," I replied.

A second later, a young woman, maybe five or so years older than us, passed us by and said, "You two are such a cute couple."

We both tried to utter something, but everything came out as unintelligible. I think I muttered something like, "Not boyfriends."

Whatever we said, she passed us on her way out of the theater. I just looked at Mario, and we burst out laughing.

When we got into Mario's car, he reached for the glove compartment. It snapped open, revealing a rectangle gift wrapped in The Grinch wrapping paper.

"Before I forget, I got you something," Mario exclaimed.

"You didn't need to...," I started.

"I wanted to," he cut me off and handed me the gift.

I tore off the Grinch's head as fast as I could, revealing three bars of chocolate. One was sea salt caramel. Another was hazelnut and milk chocolate. The last was dark chocolate and raspberry.

My mouth started watering before I had the chance to say anything. I felt this strong urge to rip all of them open and gorge myself. But before I did, I remembered the importance of self-control.

"Thank you, these all look so amazing," I said. "Do you want one?"

"I was hoping you would ask!" He smirked.

"What kind do you want?" I asked.

"No, what kind do you want?" he replied. "It is your gift."

"Okay, then...sea salt caramel it is," I exclaimed.

"Great choice," he said as I started unwrapping the chocolatey goodness.

Session #14

THE WEEK AFTER THE movie, Mario picked me up for youth group. We'd decided we wanted to get something to eat before we headed over to church. Of course, we beelined for The Golden Skillet. I was craving one of their signature cinnamon rolls oozing with all its warm and gooey icing. Mario ordered the same thing; he loved those cinnamon rolls. I also was craving some clarity about the hand holding.

As our waitress sat us, I broached the topic, "So, I've been thinking about the movie."

"Oh, yeah? What about it?" he asked.

"Well, of course, I had a great time. But I guess I was just wondering why you held my hand?" I said hesitantly.

"Oh... well... I guess I just felt like we were sharing something magical. I saw a tear in your eye, and I wanted to comfort you. And I was so happy I got to see my first gay movie in theaters. I got to see it with my best friend," he stated.

"Your best friend?" I asked, my voice quivering with uncertainty.

He took my comment differently from how I imagined it. I thought we were headed somewhere beyond being just friends. His response indicated that wasn't the case, "Yeah, you are my best friend, silly. Of course, you are!"

I wanted to believe the way he was saying "silly" was flirting, but I forced myself to think otherwise. More than anything, I did not want to ruin this friendship or make it awkward.

"Yeah, I know. You're my best friend too. I mean, you are basically my only friend," I joked.

He gave a little chuckle and stated, "Come on, Jason! You have more friends than me. What about all the people in band? Don't you have to start summer practices, soon?"

And, just like that, we were onto another conversation.

Next week's basketball came in a flash. Mario told me the team could make the playoffs if they won their game. I wasn't too sure what playoffs meant, but I knew winning was good. If winning meant I got to see his signature smile; I would be yelling until I lost my voice.

The first game came quickly. All week, Mario wouldn't stop talking about how excited but nervous he was to play. All he wanted was to impress everyone and show he could play even though he was a sophomore. I just hoped all the practicing would pay off. I'll admit. I was still not the biggest fan of his basketball career, especially after I learned just *how much* practice he would be doing. But I knew he loved it, so I tried my best to love it, too.

I'd convinced some people from youth group to go to the game with me. I thought about sitting in the student section, but I had no idea how to do any of the cheers. I also had very little interest in learning them. But I also thought it would be less suspicious if I showed up with a group of people he knew from church, instead of by myself. I doubt anyone would figure out I was there because we were queer, but I felt like I needed additional cover.

I grabbed a drink, a sour candy rope, and some popcorn from the concession stands, and our group found a spot in the stands. We made it just in time. The players stretched and practiced passing. A moment later, Mario ran near us. Our group erupted into cheers. And he looked over with that smile at us and waved. I felt like our eyes locked on each other for just a moment, and his smile grew just a tad more.

The time he committed to practicing was worth it. Again, I don't know much about basketball, and I am a bit biased. But he played beautifully. It seemed so effortless. He just ran down the court and scored. He could shoot the ball from further away, and he could do... what was it called... a layup? It basically seemed like he was the team leader. And I'll add this. The view of him in his uniform, with those shorts, was not bad. The score was not even that close. We won 76 to 53. Mario scored just over twenty of those points.

He found us after the game, and my vocal cords hurt. I yelled and yelled for him and the rest of the team. I learned a few of the chants through osmosis, I guess. Nonetheless, I tried my best to welcome him, "Hey, Mario! Great game!"

"Hey, all! Thank you so much for coming," Mario beamed. "It was so great to see you all."

The group slowly started to disperse as everyone said goodbye. A few folks went around giving everyone a little hug. Everyone had wide smiles on their faces. Eventually, it was just Mario and me.

"Well, ready to go?" Mario asked me.

"Yup!" I replied as we turned and headed straight for his car.

"Too bad your parents had to work," I blurted out. "I bet they would have loved to see it."

"Yeah, I'd like to think so," Mario replied. "I think they still wish I'd look for a job. And start buying my own things."

We didn't talk much about his family's financial struggles. Every once and a while, I would offer to help, talk to our pastor about doing a collection or have my family invite them over for dinner. Mario always insisted they were fine, but I could tell they were struggling.

"Anyway, want to come over to my house for a bit? They'll be working pretty late," Mario continued.

"Sure, sounds great!" I exclaimed.

In the blink of an eye, we were pulling into his driveway. Mario basically hopped out of his car, and I followed him.

"I'm so happy," he yelled as we entered his house.

"Yeah, I bet!" I replied enthusiastically. "You should be. You were amazing."

"Yeah, it was a good game," he said as he shut the door. He paused for a moment, looking down at the ground, "but it is more than that, too."

"Oh?" I said.

Then, he looked up at me. And he said clearly and confidently, "I am happy with you. You make me so happy, Jason."

I might have been in shock. I failed to remember how to move or talk. All I could do was see the enthusiasm and sense of euphoria on Mario's face. Mario continued, "I lied to you. I didn't hold your hand at the movie because I was happy to be with my best friend. I couldn't resist the opportunity to touch you.

And I can barely contain my feelings right now. I want to kiss you."

"I... you do?" I muttered.

"Yes, Jason, I do. And I think you want to kiss me too," he continued.

"I... I do," I responded. And he stepped toward me. Our lips touched—a sweet little peck. He hugged me, and I hugged him back.

"I thank God every day he put you in my life," he whispered and went in for another kiss. Bliss.

Session #15

A FTER OUR FIRST KISS, we officially decided we were secret boyfriends. At first, I thought some magical change would happen overnight. That didn't quite happen. Of course, some things changed. But I had thought we would be kissing and holding hands all the time. It didn't happen as much as I would have liked. We still both didn't want anyone to know, so we kept our displays of affection out of sight of the public. We were already spending as much time with each other as we could, going to youth group meetings and hanging out regularly. Of course, Mario was busy with basketball, work, and studying. So, the amount of time we could spend with each other did not change much. Other than a quick peck here and there, not too much changed in our routine at first until summer saved us from school.

When summer vacation arrived, Mario started ordering his normal toasted marshmallow latte iced. I supposed summers reminded him of campfires and making smores. But more often than not, he only drank water. Athletes need proper hygiene, he would say.

The whole summer was magical. Sadly, Mario picked up a few more shifts at work, but we were spending so much more time with each other. I felt like pinching myself constantly. I had a boyfriend in the summer, and we could just enjoy all of it.

Being the star athlete that he was, Mario liked running in the summer. It was the best way for him to stay in shape for cross-country, which in turn helped him stay in shape for the basketball season.

Early in the summer, Mario decided it would be fun to run together. Clearly, we had drastically different definitions of fun, but I did want to hang out more with him.

The first run was torture. We had met at his place, and he promised he would go slow for me. Turned out we had dramatically different definitions of slow. After the first block, I was huffing and puffing. He looked over to me. There was no sweat on his face. I could already feel some moisture working its way down my back.

He slowed to a stop, "You okay?"

"Yeah," I forced myself to say in between breaths. "Just a bit out of shape."

"No, you aren't, babe," I replied. "You probably are just not used to running in the hot sun like me."

I had not even caught my breath yet, and he had already knocked the wind out of me with one word. Babe? He'd never said that to me before.

"Babe?" I replied with a bit of shock and a lot of excitement. "That's new."

"Yeah, I guess it is," Mario stated. "How do you like it?"

"Hmmm...," I paused for a moment, mostly to build the suspense. "I like it, but I get to call you it too, babe."

"Of course, you can, babe," Mario responded.

"Deal, babe," I laughed.

"Okay, now we have that settled, babe," He said, putting a little emphasis on "babe." "What if we just do a couch to five K training thing then?"

"What's that?" I asked.

"Basically, we will start with walking and a few moments of jogging. Then, over the month, we will add in more jogging and eventually running," He replied.

"But you won't really get a workout then?" I protested.

"Don't worry about it. I'll run circles around you if I need to," he said, and a sly smirk crept onto his face.

"Shouldn't be too hard," I said.

"Seriously though, I want to spend time with you, and I need to run," Mario said. "Heck, maybe I'll convince you to join the cross-country team by the end of the summer."

"Well, if you are sure, let's do this couch to five K thing," I answered. "But I think we already did the running part for today and just need to walk."

He laughed, "Okay, we'll start it tomorrow."

For a few weeks, we met and ran. Usually, we would get a little treat afterwards. I usually told Mario I needed a reward for improving so much. He laughed and agreed. We usually ended up somewhere with ice cream, talking, and laughing.

One day, after we ran for two minutes straight and I was positive my lungs would explode, Mario slowed down practically to a stop. "My parents are gone today," He exclaimed. "So, you're going to need to get home, shower, and come over to my house.

"Yeah?" I asked. "What have you planned?"

"You'll see. It is a surprise," Mario laughed. "Just give me about an hour."

Now, you might be thinking he had planned something sexual, but I knew Mario too well by then. We wouldn't be doing anything sexual, although I thought about what sex with him would be like plenty of times.

I arrived at his house, feeling fresh and smelling good. I made sure I put on the cologne he likes. As soon as he opened the door, I could tell what he had planned. On their kitchen table, he had spread newspapers out. I could see paintbrushes sticking out of a few cups.

Before I could say anything, he said, "I thought it would be fun to paint something together."

I didn't really know what to say, so something stupid slipped out, "I'm not really good at painting."

"Me neither, babe," he exclaimed. "That's what makes it fun."

It hit me hard. My boyfriend had just planned a cute little surprise date. I smiled and asked, "Well, what are we going to paint?"

"We could just paint whatever we want," Mario said. "But I also printed out instructions for how to paint a beautiful sunset on a beach."

"Let's do that," I exclaimed. "Because I would love to watch a sunset with you someday."

"Sounds good!" He said.

Just then, the smell hit me. "What's cooking?" I asked.

"Oh, I was just making some arroz con pollo, chicken and rice for us in case we wanted to eat something," he replied.

"It smells so good," I said. "And I'm so hungry after running."

Within a minute, we sat down and started reading the instructions for the sunset-painting session. At first, we both proceeded cautiously, meticulously planning every single stroke. Slowly, we built more confidence, and our strokes became more fluid. Until Mario reached for a new brush, his elbow accidentally hit the cup of dirty water. After a few wobbles, the cup tipped over, and water went everywhere.

"Oh, shit," he said, jumping up to grab some paper towels. "I can't believe I did that!"

"Yeah, I'm surprised it wasn't me," I called after him as I got up to help.

"Exactly! I spent so much time focusing on you that I forgot about me," he retorted with a laugh.

We cleaned up the mess, and my stomach growled, giving away how hungry I was. We laughed together, and Mario asked, "Babe, you want to eat and then come back to this? The arroz con pollo should be done soon."

"Yeah, sounds good to me," I answered.

"I guess we'll eat on the couch," he said, looking down at the beautiful mess we'd created.

The arroz con pollo made my taste buds sing. It warmed my belly and my heart. I still have the painting in my room at my parents' home.

At least we saw the most beautiful sunset together before he went to heaven.

Session #16

A ARON,

I could run for about two minutes straight when Mario saw the advertisement for Big Rapids Pride. Within seconds of him sending me the information about it, we had finalized our plans.

The day came. Sweat poured from my forehead as I pushed the lawn mower over the last stretch of tall grass. The summer sun beat down on me, but I couldn't help but think about Pride in Big Rapids. I had so much to do to prepare. Shower, obviously. I bought a new deodorant that I wanted to try out. I had a new outfit. The pink shorts were perhaps a *little* shorter than I had ever worn before, plus a black T-shirt with these little white speckles. I hope Mario liked it.

Mario picked me up around four o'clock. His smile greeted me like always. I hopped in and exclaimed, "Hey, babe! You ready for this?"

"I am so ready for this! I've been thinking about it all day," He replied. "How are you feeling?"

"Good! But maybe a massive mixture of excitement and nervousness," I responded.

"Got a bunch of butterflies in your stomach?" he laughed.

"Yeah, I guess so," I laughed back.

"What are you the most excited about?" he asked.

"I've never seen a drag queen before," I answered. "I hope we see one!"

"Oh, that would be cool!" he exclaimed.

"What about you?" I asked. "What do you want to do?"

"I saw they were going to have fireworks. Do you want to stay for that?" he asked.

"Yes, I love fireworks," I said.

As we made our way to Pride, we laughed and sang along to the radio. I can't really explain it, but I just felt so easy around him. Before we knew it, we were turning the corner and saw the Big Rapids Pride sign, complete with rainbows and sparkles. A split second later, my heart sank along with all my built-up excitement. Protesters. We should have known there would be people to yell, to scream, and to tell us we were going to hell. But we hadn't thought about the possibility. During the whole ride, we kept talking about everything we wanted to experience. We listened to pump up music. We wondered if we would see a drag queen or lesbians kissing. We wanted to get rainbow stickers that we could hide in his car. We wanted to dance. We wanted to be filled with love. We wanted to show others our...well, I'm not sure we called it love yet, at least not openly.

The protesters should have just punched us right in the gut. It would have been less painful.

"Hey, as long as I am with you, I'm happy, babe," Mario said, noticing me staring at the protesters for a second too long. "And they don't know us. Only God knows us. And God is one hundred percent okay with us and our sexualities."

How did he always know what to say? I sighed, "Okay, let's do this."

As we approached the entrance, the protestors' disturbing chats grew louder. I gritted my teeth and prepared myself to walk past. I saw the back of their obnoxious shirts—a basic black arrow pointed down, and the text read "Exit, Not Entrance." They must think more about gay sex than I do, I thought.

Then, I saw them. The counter-protesters. A fine-sized group of people were holding up signs which said we are loved. One sign said, "God loves you." Another had the words "Have a Blessed Pride" written on it. My smile instantly returned as I felt their warmth and their love. I knew which "side" I would find God on.

Then, I saw her. Her hair was bright red. It was so bright I wondered how I could have missed it. Dressed in clerical garb and a rainbow stole, she held a sign which simply said, "Free Hugs." And I knew I wanted one.

I turned to Mario. He anticipated what I was going to say and exclaimed, "I want one too!"

We rushed over to her and simply opened our arms. She did the same. All three of us embraced. She smelled of lavender, instantly comforting me. We held onto each other for a while. And we held on. I felt Mario tremble a little. When we let go, I saw a little twinkle in his eye. She said, "You are so loved. Have the most beautiful Pride."

"Thank you!" I said, "It's our first time."

"All the more reason to celebrate!" She said, "My church has a booth inside. We have some candy and other little gifts. Stop by if you want."

"Okay," I said, looking over to Mario. He had a tear running down his face. But his smile was there.

He nodded and said, "Thank you so much!"

As we were walking away, he leaned into me and said, "I am so happy we did that."

"She's the kind of Christian we have been looking for," I said.

"Absolutely," Mario uttered.

"I'm glad you got to meet her," I continued as I reached to wipe the tear off his face.

I wanted to plant one on his lips right there in front of everyone, but Mario turned to hand the person admitting folks our money.

We walked around Pride and just took it all in. I lost count of all the rainbow flags I saw. Some guys strutted around in very revealing shorts, or should I say a speedo? I'm pretty sure both Mario and I were both wondering how it all fit in there. I didn't ask Mario, but I really wanted to know. We both stared for a moment too long, and he noticed us. But I don't think he minded. It looked like he was checking out Mario, and I can't say I blame him. I knew I was walking next to one of the most attractive people here.

Suddenly, I felt like I was under a microscope. I never really felt this way before, realizing that these guys might be checking me out. They would notice me checking them out. In heteronormative Small Rapids, I just assumed no guy would ever check me out. They were all straight, pretty much. So, it never mattered how I looked or acted. But now, it did. Guys would look at me and Mario, and I suddenly felt like I did not match up to my boyfriend.

I second-guessed myself. Did I look at all attractive? Obviously, I would never look as beautiful as Mario, but would anyone ever glance my way? I felt "meh" about how I looked for a long time. I wasn't the best-looking person in the room, but I didn't completely hate how I looked. Was it enough? Would people ever think Mario and I were a couple? Or was it obvious that I was out of his league? Did they think he was generous by bringing his friend to Pride?

Mario must have noticed I was lost in my thoughts: "Are you okay?"

"Yeah," I lied. "Just trying to take it all in."

"Never had a guy stare at you like that before, huh?" Mario asked. "Besides me, of course."

At first, I wanted to yell at him. Why would he tease me right now? But his voice was serious. It shook me.

"What do you mean?" I asked.

"Speedo guy. I think he was checking you out," Mario said.

"I don't think so. He was clearly checking you out," I exclaimed.

"Well, maybe he just wanted a ménage à trois?" Mario wondered out loud.

"Maybe," I said with a shrug.

"Would you ever want to do that?" Mario asked.

"What?" I laughed.

"Would you ever want to have a threesome?" Mario clarified.

"Oh? I don't know," I replied. "How about we think about it after our first time."

Mario chuckled, "Probably for the best."

We walked around, soaking up every detail. Lesbian couples held hands as they listened to whoever was playing on stage. We walked past a little covered area labeled "the bear cave," and I made a mental note to look that up later. I saw a drag queen. She had this epic make-up; I bet you could see from a mile away. Another man with short shorts handed out condoms near one of the booths. We saw a sign for a sexually transmitted infection testing location. Lots of folks carried around what looked like orange slush to me, and Mario and I guessed they had alcohol in them. Frankly, it was all a bit overwhelming. But in a good way. One new experience after another after another. I could hardly believe there were so many people and so many things to do. So many people who were queer folks or loved us. It all reminded me of the kid in a candy shop feeling: wide eyes and wanting to try everything. Other than the orange slush, I guess.

We stopped by the pastor's church stand. In front of the stand was a large sign: Central Street United Methodist Church. An elderly Black woman asked us if she could pray for us.

"Yes, please," Mario answered.

We closed our eyes and clasped our hands. She simply said, "Lord, thank you for this beautiful day where we can celebrate all your children. Please keep these two young gentlemen safe, and always remind them they are cherished children of God. Amen."

"Amen," we said in unison.

The church had little stickers that said, "God loves queers." So, we grabbed a few of those, thanked the woman, and went on to the next thing. At that moment, I was so excited to put my sticker on. Later, I would worry someone would find out about my little sticker. With Mario, though, I felt so happy to put the sticker on. We grabbed some fries and grilled chicken sandwiches to eat. Mario reminded me we needed to drink water. We walked around in a blissful daze for another hour or so.

As the sun set, I felt the temperature drop, but the wind still felt warm. Just in time for the fireworks, we found a boulder to lean on. We sat back as the first explosion sounded. Cheers erupted, and Mario yelled in excitement. I took a quick peek, and his smile was lighting up his face. Another explosion grabbed my attention, and another round of yelling echoed through the night. Dazzling colors brightened the sky, and I wondered how in the world they created a firework that could make a rainbow. I noticed a slight pain in my face as my smile stretched further than it could possibly go. It's hard to explain how I felt, but it was as if my feet were lifting me off the ground. I was weightless, unrestrained...

I was free. My happiness could not be contained.

His hand found mine and latched on. I rubbed his thumb with mine. The fireworks kept thundering above. He tugged at me a little. I looked over at him. His eyes met mine, and somewhere in there, our lips found each other.

Session #17

MARIO AND I RARELY felt like we could go on real, public dates. Occasionally, we would drive off together to spend a day in the city. Usually, we walked around pretending to shop and imagining what we would buy if we had more money. Sometimes, we were able to get enough money together to buy some ice cream, coffee, or hot chocolate. I just loved spending time with him, laughing and chatting. I didn't mind the occasional hug or kiss when we felt like we could.

We went to this outlet mall; it was one I'd visited at least a hundred times with my family over the years. Because of that, I was always too scared to hold hands with him. We knew we might encounter folks we knew from school or their families.

During the Fall of our Junior year, something happened that caused the most turbulence in our relationship. We had to confront what and who we were. Were we, in fact, an interracial couple? Or was it interethnic? Both? I'm not sure. The difference between race and ethnicity always confuses me.

Anyway, we were walking along the sidewalk near my favorite ice cream shop. I hardly ever came to this outlet mall without getting something from there. It was just so creamy and yummy. I would even get it in winter.

It all happened so fast. Someone's car slowed down next to us. The windows slid down. That's when I heard it. A barrage of racial slurs assaulted our ears. Before I could process anything logically, my blood was already boiling. My muscles tensed up. My jaw clenched. And, like nothing happened, they sped off.

I regret how I reacted. I froze, stunned. My mind went blank. A small part of me hoped I was dreaming, but the rest of me knew better.

Mario just kept walking.

I took a few quick steps to catch up with him and simply asked, "Mario?"

"Don't worry about it," he replied with heat and a bit of venom. Startled, my mouth dropped open. I had never heard him express such anger, sadness, and pain all at once, and we shared our pain, sadness, and anger often.

"I...," I uttered.

"I don't want to talk about it, babe," Mario said more firmly. The "babe" was less cutesy than normal; it rang like an exclamation point.

"*Okay…*," I was struggling. Seriously struggling. Looking back, I wish I'd focused less on myself. When it happened, I was so concerned with my lack of understanding, with my confusion, and with my inability to decide what to do. I should have thought more about Mario and what he was trying to process.

"Actually, can we just go home?" Mario asked suddenly.

"Yeah, if that's what you want," I replied.

He simply nodded.

We drove home in silence. It nearly killed me. My mind was racing, trying to work out what I could do or say. Should I reach over to hold his hand? Maybe I should start a conversation about something totally harmless, like whether he had been practicing? Although that question might not be the most harmless, I knew he was practicing a bit less than usual. I don't think he liked being around the people he normally played with as much anymore. I rubbed my face in my hands. I felt stupid for having no clue what to do. Again, I foolishly make it all about me.

My stomach growled loudly about five minutes from home, breaking the silence.

"Want to go to The Golden Skillet?" he asked.

"I would, if you're okay with it," I said.

"Yeah, I could go for a cinnamon roll," he stated. We loved stress eating together at Golden Skillet. Was that all this was? Did he want to stress eat?

We were greeted with the warm, friendly service we'd become accustomed to. When we sat down in our booth, Mario's eyes darted down at the table. He just stared at the menu—his mind clearly elsewhere. He looked up briefly to order. We both ordered our favorite gooey goodness... and then sat in silence. One minute passed by. And then two minutes. And then three. Four. Five.

I started to wonder if we were going to say anything at all. Eventually, he looked up and made eye contact. His eyes were strained like he was fighting back tears, and my heart broke. I remembered back to the moment when the pastor yelled about the sin of homosexuality, and the hurt I saw on his face. Words always leave deep scars.

I really wanted to see him happy—to see his smile. I wanted to make a joke, anything to cheer him up. But I also knew it wasn't the time or the place for levity.

Hesitantly, I spoke, "Ummm, I'm not sure what to say, but I just wanted to say I love you."

He sighed, and his face tensed. He said, "I know. I love you too."

I desperately wanted to reach my hand toward his, but I knew neither of us felt comfortable holding hands here. Strange how such simple acts like wanting to comfort someone, or wanting to hold their hands, remind you how discrimination shapes our daily lives.

I continued, "I hope you know how much I want to hold your hand and comfort you right now."

He smirked, "Yeah, I know."

"Okay, just wanted to make sure," I replied.

He sighed again, "I promise we can talk about this some other time. I just don't want to right now."

"Anything else you want to talk about?" I asked.

He laughed and exclaimed, "So, are you ever going to let me take you to a basketball game?"

"Maybe someday," I replied. "But you are going to have to explain every single thing that's happening."

"I would be honored to rid you of your basketball ignorance," he said, and I was rewarded with his smirk, which made my knees turn to jelly.

Session #18

H I Aaron,

The day had finally arrived. Mario had convinced me to go to a college basketball game with him. I agreed, and we had a great cover story. As Juniors, we needed to start thinking about college, so our date conveniently included a day out of touring the college and going to the game. The campus was beautiful and only about an hour and a half drive from our hometown. Just close enough that we could head back home if we ever needed anything, and just far enough away, we wouldn't really be running into folks from high school or our parents on a daily basis.

Fortunately, it was an untypically warm December. We grabbed our usual lattes for the drive. Before we knew it, we were on one of those official campus tours. The volunteer showed us and a bunch of other potential students around campus, pointing out the various buildings. This one is the library, which was obvious. But it was nice to learn video streaming services were readily available. We loved free things, especially food and movies. We would have done anything to save a penny or two. We thought the dorm buildings looked incredibly fancy. Recently renovated, they had this amazing food court as the cafeteria. The array of food options dazzled us: pizza, ramen noodles, spaghetti, burgers, ice cream, salads, and an assortment of cookies. I envisioned us near one of the windows, sitting and chatting about our classes and what we wanted to do for fun later. And, because our future was going to be perfect, I wasn't going to get cookie crumbs all over my shirt.

We eventually arrived at the student union. Again, I can only think of the word beautiful to describe the building and its architecture. More importantly, the tour guide listed off the many and various campus offices in the building.

To make sure everyone could hear, the guide had been yelling. They exclaimed, "Also, the union houses the Inclusive Excellence Center on campus. The university works diligently to ensure the needs of all students are met, and the Inclusive Excellence Center's main goal is to do exactly that. Within the Center, you will find veteran support services and our LGBTQ+ initiatives and programming."

I looked directly at Mario and gave a slight nod. To hear someone mention supporting queer folks was heartwarming. Mario beamed. I felt like I saw our future clearly. We walked out of the Center, laughing with other queer friends we'd made.

"The Center also has an office to support Latinx students and other people of color. Some of our students formed a Black Student Union a couple of years ago, and the Center supports their efforts," the tour guide continued.

I looked back over at Mario, and somehow, his already massive, signature smile grew even wider. Could it get any bigger? It didn't seem possible.

A few hours later, we found our way to the arena for the main event. The basketball game was fine. Without Mario, I would have understood very little of it. I mean, I understood the general concepts like dribbling down the court and trying to score. He needed to explain basically everything else, like what fouls had happened each time the whistle blew. Honestly, a few times, I lost track of which team we were supporting, and Mario kindly reminded me. I knew sports mattered to Mario, and he mattered to me. I was sure it was just a matter of time before sports mattered to me, too. I like to think he enjoyed teaching me about something he loved and had worked so hard to master.

Mostly, it was just wonderful for me to see him this happy, infinite, and infectious. It felt impossible to feel any pain or sadness when he was like this, so animated and engaged in the game. He was in his happy place. And, because he had found his, I had found mine.

The excitement remained in his voice as we drove home. He exclaimed, "That was such a wonderful day. I think I actually want to go there."

"Yeah, I could literally feel your happiness all day," I laughed.

"Did you like it too?" he asked.

"I think so. I liked the dorms and the library, alright. I'm already imagining us eating lunch in the cafeteria. And I'm really happy they explicitly support LGBTQ+ students," I replied. "But what I loved the most is how much you loved it all."

"I imagine I am going to spend a lot of time at the Inclusive Excellence, or whatever they called it, Center," Mario said. "I am especially interested in Latinx support programs."

"Yeah?" I said, and my voice must have registered some sense of shock.

Mario responded, "Of course! It will be great to have folks working to support us Hispanic folks and the struggles we go through. I don't really have many people in our little town to talk about it now."

"I guess that's true," I continued and, again, I must have still had a bit of confusion in my voice.

Mario continued, "Think of it, babe. I saw your face light up when they mentioned the LGBTQ+ support, but that's how I feel about the Hispanic support, too. I want both. I have to navigate being queer and Hispanic. I'm a queer Hispanic guy, and I often feel like I can't really be either at high school."

"What do you mean?" I asked. Sometimes, I wonder if I'm just stupid. Looking back on it, of course Mario would have had a different experience than I did. A lot of the time, I just thought about how we were the same because we were both gay. But I know now that wasn't the truth at all.

"I mean, we have talked about how we don't think we can really be out and open about our sexualities at school, yeah?" he asked.

"Yeah, of course," I responded.

"And I feel similarly about being Hispanic or Latinx," he said. "I obviously can't hide my skin color, but I feel like I am still hiding part of who I am. Like, people love that I can speak Spanish when it comes to asking about their Spanish homework, but when I speak Spanish with my parents on the phone, people just stare at me. I feel the judgement, the hypocrisy."

"So, it feels like double discrimination then?" I asked rather ineloquently. The words struggled to form.

"Yeah, I guess you could say that. I feel like people would hate me if they learned about us and how I am gay. But I also know people disdain me for my skin color; they assume I am some bad hombre when they see me coming," Mario continued.

"Like when we were at the outlet mall?" I questioned.

Mario sighed deeply, and I realized I'd likely prompted him to relive a painful moment.

Then, he nodded, "Yeah, like at the outlet mall. It doesn't happen to me as often as it happens to my parents, but it does happen. Maybe people think my parents are uneducated because they do not speak English so well, and sometimes people question whether they are legal or American. It hurts every time."

"I guess I just didn't realize this type of stuff was happening to you," I said rather solemnly. "Until I witnessed it."

"It is hard for me to talk about, and it is hard for me to talk about it with you. I know we talk about how hard it is to be queer in a homophobic society. And that's true. It just sucks. But I often want to add how I feel like my being Hispanic also impacts me daily. But—and I say this with love—you don't know what it's like to experience what I experience. The hate from being queer, and the hate from being Hispanic. I worry about people discriminating against me being queer, and I also must consistently navigate microaggressions about me being Hispanic. And I worry the folks who help me navigate racism will abandon me if they know

I was queer, and I worry that White gay folks might discriminate against me for being brown,"

Mario shared with so much poise. I know how angry he gets about anti-queer hate, so I imagine he must feel the same anger when it comes to the discrimination he faces as a Hispanic person.

The electricity between us felt new, like Mario had just let something off his chest—something he wanted to tell me but struggled to figure out how. It reminded me of how it felt when we came out to each other. It was different, of course. I knew Mario was Hispanic, but I did not know how much thought and energy he had put into navigating his identity as a queer Hispanic man. But, still, suddenly, there seemed to be less tension between us, even though moments ago, I would have said we had always been so relaxed around each other.

I thought about the moments when a teacher seemed surprised when he stepped into their advanced placement class. I always interpreted their reaction was simply because they didn't realize he was smart in addition to being a star athlete, but maybe they didn't expect him in their class because of his... Latinx-ness? Is that a word? I'm not sure what word to use to describe it.

Eventually, I said, "Thank you for sharing, Mario. I sense this has been weighing on you. I don't really know what to say other than I appreciate you trusting me with this."

"I've wanted to tell you. After all, I see us being a thing for quite some time," Mario said with a quick and exaggerated wink. "I just wasn't sure how you would react."

"I'm happy you shared," I continued, hoping I was reacting in a decent enough manner. "I'm sure it was not easy."

"No, it's never easy being vulnerable with others, but I guess that's what it takes to get close to someone," he said. At the time, I couldn't agree more.

Session #19

MARIO AND I CONTINUED to date in secret. I beamed every time I thought about our relationship. But, once we started dating, I realized I had zero romantic bones in my body. Mario had at least one. One Saturday night in January, I went over to his house to study and work on homework with him. At least, that's what I thought we'd be doing. Instead, I arrived and immediately smelled something incredible. He'd made chicken enchiladas for us. I am obviously biased, but they were amazing. My taste buds danced, and I let out a guttural groan of pleasure.

He knew how to do those small little things, which showed how thoughtful he was, how much he cared, and how much he adored me. One day, he picked me up for school and already had a caramel latte waiting for me. Another day, he had one of the gooey cinnamon rolls waiting for me.

And I *know* dating and romance is not a competition, but I felt like I was losing. I wanted to show him how much I cared for him. I texted him one night a week or so before Valentine's Day, "Don't make any plans for Valentine's Day. I'm taking care of it all."

"Oh, what do you have in mind?" He texted back.

"It is a surprise," I answered.

"Oh, I love a man who takes charge," he responded. I sensed his smirk through the phone.

"Stop," I wrote. "Just be ready for an epic date."

"Yes, sir," he wrote back.

Valentine's Day arrived before I knew it. The anticipation was killing me. I knew I had a great idea for a date, and today would be special for us. Luckily, Valentine's Day fell on a Friday, so we would not have to worry about school the next day. Even more importantly, Mario did not have a basketball game, and the weather was perfect: no clouds or rain was forecast. The temperature wouldn't go much above seventy-five degrees Fahrenheit. Again, perfect.

I took a lot of time to get ready. I wanted to look as good as I felt. I bought a brand-new T-shirt and shorts, and I also got this rustic-smelling cologne. I hardly ever did my hair, but I used some texturing gel.

Mario picked me up right on time at six o'clock. Even though I planned the night, Mario still wanted to drive. I'm pretty sure he thought I would get us killed with my "awful" driving someday. I had just received my license, so he wasn't wrong; I sucked at driving. I didn't want to fight about it. He loved to drive, and I simply didn't.

I knew I was going to get a strange look when I got into his car with my backpack. Eyebrow raised, he asked, "What is the backpack for?"

"You'll see," I responded. "You ready?"

"Yes!" He answered. "I'm so excited to find out what you've been hiding from me for like two weeks."

"Has it really been two weeks?" I asked.

"Yes, it has!" he replied. "I've been counting the minutes!"

"Must have been hard," I joked.

"Come on, babe! Just tell me where we're going," he said.

"I'll give you directions, but I'm not telling you just yet," I chuckled. I enjoyed watching him squirm just a little too much.

"Fine!" he exclaimed, faking exasperation.

We drove off. Small Rapids soon disappeared behind us as I directed Mario to drive towards a really wooded area in the country. Mario must have assumed we were not going far, because he asked, "Okay, really, where are we going?"

"Don't worry about it," I replied. "We'll be there soon."

"This is starting to feel a bit like a horror movie," he said, laughing. "I'm picking up a seriously 'Children of the Corn' vibe."

"The sun's still out!" I exclaimed.

"Texas Chainsaw Massacre, then," he continued.

"Babe, we don't live in Texas," I chuckled.

"Are there any horror movies about Valentine's Day?" he asked suddenly. He glimpsed at me, and I pointed to the road ahead.

"I have no idea," I replied with a shrug. "I hate horror movies."

"Yeah, me too," he said. "Well, mostly, I just can't bring myself to watch hack-and-slash films."

A moment later, I spotted the dirt road I was searching for. I said, "Okay, turn right up there onto the dirt road."

"Seriously?" He frowned. "You're sure we aren't in a horror movie?"

"Don't let your guard down," I chuckled as he started to make the turn. "When we get to the end of the road, you'll need to find a parking spot."

"Where are we?" he asked again.

"A park, you'll see," I answered finally. "I hope no one else thought of this place."

The park's sign slowly came into view: Presidio Park.

"Presidio Park?" He asked.

"Yes, babe. That's exactly what the sign says," I answered sarcastically.

"Never heard of it," he stated.

"I don't think too many people have," I said. "That's what I'm hoping, at least."

Sure enough, no other cars were parked there. As soon as we parked, I hopped out with my backpack. With much enthusiasm, I asked, "Did you remember to bring water?"

"Yeah, I did," He replied as he held up his bottle so I could see it. "We going for a hike?"

"Yup!" I declared.

"Sounds great," he answered. "I love getting away in nature."

"I know," I said. "And we are headed to my favorite place of all time."

"Yeah?" he asked.

"Yup, and we better get moving. It's about an hour hike," I said.

"Let's get going then," he said. And off we went. For an hour, we pointed out various critters together. Squirrels frolicked around. Birds sang. Rabbits dashed toward their homes. The hike always goes by quicker with company, and so we arrived in what only felt like a few minutes.

"Wow, look at that view," Mario exclaimed. We had just arrived in the clearing: our destination. We stood on a natural overlook and only saw forest as far as we could see. Whenever I entered the area, I felt a total sense of calm. The only sounds were an occasional bird chirping. The air smelled pristine, and I automatically took a deep, refreshing breath. This place always made me feel alive.

"Yeah, I love it up here," I answered, taking my backpack off and starting to open it. I made peanut butter sandwiches. I didn't want to add jelly because I didn't want the bread to get damp. Not sure if it's a real thing, but I recalled having mushy bread with my peanut butter and jelly sandwiches when I was a kid. I also brought along a large blanket that we soon had laid out over the ground.

"You hungry?" I asked.

"Yeah," he answered.

"The hike can work up an appetite," I said.

"But, wow, was it all worth it," he exclaimed, still looking at the view.

"Just wait until sunset," I replied.

He reached around my waist, and I leaned into him. The sun slowly set as I listened to his breathing: slow, steady, and calm. At first, some yellows and oranges appeared on the horizon. Then, some pinks and little purples joined. The colors grew larger and larger. The hues radiated toward us, and we felt their warmth.

"This is beautiful," Mario whispered. "Happy Valentine's Day, babe."

"Happy Valentine's Day," I echoed. He leaned in and kissed the top of my head, and I instantly worried he would taste the hair gel I'd used. But he didn't complain. I turned toward him and kissed him back. The kissing grew more and more intense. Mario reached down to pull off his shirt, and I watched in amazement as he pulled it over his head until he got stuck. Somehow, he just couldn't get the shirt over his head. If I didn't know better, I would have guessed he just wanted me to see all the muscles he had been building. And it worked. His tight chest and abdominal muscles basically held my gaze like a fly attracted to light. He flailed around for a moment, and I couldn't help but let out a little cackle.

"Help me, babe!" he exclaimed. I grabbed onto his shirt and pulled with all my might. Finally, he wiggled out of his shirt.

"Looking good," I said, and he knew I was just staring at him.

"Your turn," he replied slyly as he reached toward my shirt.

"What? No," I answered.

"Why?" He asked as his hands all but snapped back to his side.

I thought about it for a moment. Why was I suddenly feeling shy around him? He had always made me feel safe. I let out a huge sigh when I realized what I was thinking. Looking at his body, his toned and muscular body, I knew it was because I didn't feel as attractive as him. And I knew I shouldn't keep it to myself. I nervously whispered, "I just don't feel very good-looking."

I waited, bracing myself for whatever he was about to say. His eyebrows narrowed, and he tilted his head to the side a bit. What was that look? Confusion? He slowly but firmly stated the following: "Babe, listen to me. You are beautiful."

"But I..." I protested.

He cut me off, "But nothing. You have an amazing body. Why else do you think I checked you out that first night at Youth Group? More importantly, you are a beautiful person, inside and out. You have a kind, generous, loving, and beautiful soul."

"Really?" I asked tentatively.

"Yes, really. I love you, Jason Marshall," he answered as his signature smile emerged little by little. "Do you believe me?"

"I do. Of course, I do," I answered.

"And... Jason," his voice lingered in the warm night air.

"Oh, of course, I love you too," I replied. "I love you so dang much!"

"Can I kiss you then?" he asked, leaning closer and closer to me.

"Of course," I replied right before he gave me a sweet peck on the lips.

After he released me, I tentatively reached down to grab the bottom of my shirt. But the closer my hands got, the faster they moved. Within a second, my shirt was up over my head and tossed to the side.

"See? Beautiful," he stated, his voice warm yet unwavering.

"Oh, shucks," I said as I suddenly felt my cheeks heating.

He reached in for another peck, and then he nonchalantly said, "I don't ever want to hear you making fun of my boyfriend, okay?"

"Okay," I replied, now feeling a little embarrassed for confessing that I felt less attractive than him.

"You are attractive, alright?" he continued.

"Okay," I stated.

"Say it," he demanded.

"Oh, come on," I said.

"No more kisses until you say it," he whispered as he leaned in and rudely pulled away.

"Really?" I asked.

"Really. Say it," he demanded again.

"I'm… attractive," I uttered as quietly as I could.

"What was that? I couldn't hear you," he exclaimed.

"I. Am. Attractive," I said more forcefully.

"Huh?" he replied.

"I'm attractive," I exclaimed.

"Again!" he demanded.

"I'm attractive!" I yelled.

"Again!" he insisted.

"I am uber attractive!" I shouted at the top of my lungs.

He practically lunged at me, scooped me up in an embrace, and planted a wet one right on my lips. We rolled, and he landed on top of me.

"And don't you forget it," he said calmly.

"I won't," I replied as my stupid tear duct told me I needed that. I needed the affirmation. I needed to feel good about myself. I needed to love myself.

"So, I don't think we've ever really talked about how far we want to take things," Mario stated as he moved to kiss my neck.

"No, I guess we haven't," I replied, suddenly noticing how dark it was getting. The sun was about to slip beyond the horizon.

"Is just kissing good for now?" he asked.

"Yeah, I really like kissing," I answered. He kissed me again; this time, it was a bit deeper. Tongues were involved.

After a couple of blissful minutes, Mario must have realized how dark it was getting, too.

"It is getting pretty dark, babe," he said as a cool gust of wind blew over us.

My whole body shivered, and I noticed he did, as well. We both reached for our shirts and put them back on.

"Yeah, I don't think we should take anything further tonight," I laughed.

"I guess not," he said.

We packed up the blanket as quickly as we could and started heading back down the trail. Within minutes, everything was pitch black. We pulled our phones out to use as lights. Even then, we could barely see.

"I told you this was going to be a horror movie," Mario jested.

"You're going to fight off the axe murderer so I can get away, right?" I asked.

"No, babe. You're on your own," he answered.

"That's rude. I'm your boyfriend," I exclaimed.

"Okay, fine. We'll take the axe murderer together," he declared.

"Okay. Sounds good. At least we will die together," I said.

"That's the most romantic thing I've ever heard," he joked.

I decided that day I might just have at least one romantic bone in my body.

Of course, as I think back, I'm flooded with conflicting emotions. I am so happy I spent that kind of time with Mario, and I cherish those memories. But I'm sad, too. I still miss him and think about him all the time. I just can't forget him, and I don't want to. I relive the pain again whenever I remember the happiness. I also wonder if I will ever be in that kind of relationship again. I wonder if I'll ever meet someone I love enough to bring here—my happy place.

Maybe someday?

Session #20

ARON,

I was wondering if we could talk about something a little taboo for today's session. I hope it's okay.

You see, I am still a virgin. And I feel anxious about it. I generally just think I am scared to have sex. Mario and I never took it all the way. We had talked about it, of course, but we never acted on it.

Mario awkwardly brought it up one night after our Valentine's Day date. We were on our usual date at the Golden Skillet before our youth group meeting.

After ordering his cinnamon roll, he leaned in close. Quietly, almost too quietly, he asked, "Can we talk about something?"

"Yeah, why?" I hesitated.

"Well, I've been thinking about our relationship ever since Valentine's Day," he continued.

"Okay," I said with a hint of nervous anticipation.

"Well, we never finished our conversation about... how far we want to go," he stated.

My face flushed up right away. Of course, he was right. We never finished our little chat. I instinctively looked around to see if anyone else noticed the question. But as usual, the room was too loud for anyone to hear what anyone else was discussing. So, I responded, trying to move past my initial shock, "Oh? And what have you been thinking about it?"

"Like, are we waiting for marriage? Or do we want to try it sooner?" he asked calmly.

He was clearly much more ready to have this discussion than I was. I, of course, had had many unholy thoughts about him, but I never considered just going all the way. So, I told him just that. Honesty is the best policy.

"I guess I never really thought about it. I don't really know. I mean, I'm not even really sure how we are supposed to, you know, do it." I replied. "What do you think?"

"Well, I really want to try with you. And I don't really want to wait for marriage, especially since we could lose the right to marry at some point," he explained.

Sadly, I knew he was right. We barely had the right to marry. And I knew I wanted to marry him, but I must confess I wasn't all too sure what our marriage would look like. No one even knew about us. How could we plan this epic, extravagant wedding? We had a lot of work to do before then. Could we wait?

"I know what you mean," I replied solemnly.

"But I want it to be special. No hooking up in a gas station bathroom, not that there's anything wrong with that. But it's not what I want for us. I want us to be committed to each other, and I just want our first time to be magical. Or extremely awkward as we try to figure out what to do. I just don't know if I want to wait so long," he explained.

"I want it to be special too, like some epic romantic thing we plan. Either after our wedding or a special occasion like prom," I said.

Luckily, that changed the conversation. Mario asked, "So, you think we will ever go to prom together?"

"I don't know. I want to, but I'd also be just as happy to skip it and simply be with you," I said. "I don't want everyone looking at us."

"I do want to dance with you," Mario said but then took a quick jab at my dancing skills, "I'll just have to teach you first."

And that's how our conversations about sex went. I guess you would say we did want to save it for a meaningful moment—a moment we would remember forever. Sometimes Mario changed his mind and wanted to save it for marriage. Back then, I had fully planned on marrying him, so it might have turned out that way. At other times, I hoped I could persuade him the night of graduation or our anti-prom night could be another magic time. Maybe for my birthday? Or his? Such naive thoughts.

I would have felt comfortable trying with him. It would be the first time for both of us, and we cared for each other. If something didn't work or we messed up, we'd talk through it. We would laugh about it, and we would try it again. I craved that level of comfort with someone else—the feeling of being open, honest, and non-judgmental.

I recently learned about the term demisexual. Basically, it means someone needs to form a close emotional bond with someone before they can find them attractive. I think I've also heard about it being like only being physically attracted to smart people, but it might be a different term. I'm not sure. I don't know if that's what I am or how I feel, but I do know I really don't have a desire to have sex with anyone right now. A part of me thinks it's because I am psyching myself out about still being a virgin. A part of me thinks I am nervous about messing up or not being good. But another part of me knows I want to know someone and be in love with them before I sleep with them. But maybe that's just being old-fashioned and unrealistic. *What if my unconscious is still saving it for a romantic night with Mario?*

I mention this because I have been wanting to try dating again. I know Mario would want me to be happy, and I know I cannot live the rest of my life always thinking about him and wanting him back. I must be realistic. I need to enjoy life again. I need to find happiness. Living in the past and wishing something different had happened will get me nowhere anytime soon.

But I don't really know how to meet up with someone—someone with whom I can develop a deep relationship. One like the one I had with Mario. Every time I try a dating app, I feel like I find guys who only want to hook up. I struggle to introduce myself to people. I don't really know what to say or when to say it. Even when I am talking with a guy, I still feel like I am not sure what is just being nice or what is flirting. It's all really, really confusing.

I also don't want to be hurt again. How can I develop a close, comfortable relationship with someone and not worry that I will lose them? I know I just said I'm working to live a life now without Mario, but I don't want to feel any more pain. I have been thinking about it quite a bit, and I am more and more convinced that I feel comfortable being unhappy and miserable. I do not trust happiness; it feels like a lie, and at any moment, all the happiness could be sucked out of my life, leaving me feeling hollow, numb, and devoid of any emotion.

Session #21

H I AARON,

My brain hurts whenever I think about how different my life would be if the shooting never happened. What would our lives be like now? Would Mario and I be at the same college? Would we have taken our relationship to the next step? Would we still be dating? Would we be out? The questions always circulate—an annoying buzz flying by my ear.

After Mario brought up sex, I spent nights tossing and turning about whether we would be able to get married. I envisioned us at the altar. I imagined my family was nowhere to be found. But sometimes I saw their smiles and heard them saying they loved us. Now, I will never be about to know how they would react, at least not with Mario.

Life was on the brink of being very different for us when the shooting ripped him out of my life. One night, we were hanging out at his house, watching television, eating popcorn, and laughing. We usually met at his house, because his parents always had to work. Suddenly, Mario sparked a conversation, one we seemed to know how to avoid until that very moment.

"Hey, babe, I've been thinking more about it. Coming out," Mario started the conversation, a little more hesitation in his voice than usual.

"Yeah, what about it?" I asked.

"Let's say we wanted to. How do you want to do it? All at once? Or only tell a few people first?" he continued, looking me in the eyes and reaching for my hand. At this point in our relationship, we had a little tradition. Whenever we needed to talk about something difficult or something we'd fought about before, we would embrace each other to help us remember we were in it together. Whatever the issue, we could confront it as a team.

"Oh, I hadn't really thought about it too much. But I guess I would want to tell our parents first," I said, letting him pull me into his firm arms. He squeezed me gently, and I returned the favor.

When he spoke next, I could tell he was already fighting back a tear or two. A part of me, and not a small one, was shocked he was the one who brought the conversation up again. He let out a deep breath and replied, "Yeah, I guess. That makes the most sense, doesn't it?"

"I think so unless you want to tell people at school first," I said. "But I want to do whatever you are the most comfortable with."

"Who would you think about telling at school?" he asked gently.

"Maybe Ms. Mullen?" I suggested, tentatively.

"The librarian?" he inquired.

"Yeah, the librarian," I replied, "Remember you noticed a few queer-themed books on the shelf a couple of weeks ago. Everyone is always talking about how they think she is a lesbian."

"Oh yeah, I remember. She could be a good choice," Mario stated, but I could tell he was unconvinced and, frankly, probably unsure about telling anyone. Sometimes, I worry I'd pushed him too far on the coming out issue. I knew he was nervous about it; I was too. But I wanted people to know how much I had fallen for him.

"But I know how important your mom and dad are to you," I shifted the conversation back to where I knew Mario needed the most comfort.

"Yeah, I... I don't want to feel like I am lying to them. And I don't like making up stories about what we are doing when we... you know, fool around a bit," he started, and I just wanted to listen as I held him for support. "But I am just so worried about what they will do. It is hard enough already for them as they try to fit into this, let's be honest, white town. They work too many jobs and still struggle to make ends meet. And they feel barely included at church as it is, and it is probably the most diverse and inclusive church here. I don't want to disappoint them, and I don't want to make their lives any more difficult."

One of his tears landed on me as they trickled down the side of his face. I was holding him as tightly as I could as he trembled, and I felt a familiar pain in the corner of my eye. Why did this have to be so hard?

"I know, babe. I know," I said as calmly and steadily as I could.

"I know you want to come out. I do, too, but I'm so scared," he exclaimed.

I just continued to soothe him, saying, "I know. Me too. But I think we'll know when the time is right."

A week later, Mario rushed up to me after basketball practice. Smiling, he took a breath and blurted out, "Okay! I've been praying about it, and I think we just need to take the leap."

"What?" I was puzzled at first.

He pulled out a folded-up piece of lined paper from his pocket and handed it over to me. But then he quickly added, "Wait until we get to the car to open it."

On our way to youth group, he explained, "It's a coming out letter to my parents. Well, a draft of it at least. I wanted you to read it to see what you think because I want to tell them about us. And, well, I wanted your permission first."

"Really?" I said the shock in my voice must have been obvious.

"I know it's quick, especially given how our last conversation about it went. But I started writing the letter to process what I was thinking about it all, and I basically convinced myself we should do it," he started.

"You are really persuasive, babe," I tried to joke because my heart had skipped several beats.

"I am still so scared about this, but I just woke up the other day. I was thinking about you, of course. And I was thinking about how happy we are and how much I just freaking adore you so much. And I need them to know. It's just that simple. I don't want to hide anymore, and I don't want to hide you. I need to know if they can accept it. I need to take the plunge," he excitedly word-vomited at me.

I smiled mostly because of how cute he was when he was this excited but also because I was so happy to know I was no longer the only one in the relationship who would word vomit.

That was two days before the shooting. I hadn't even had time to read the letter and talk with him about it. I still have the letter, hidden in my room. It was so beautiful; I could never get rid of it.

Dear Mom and Dad,

I have something important to tell you, and I hope you'll both be happy for me. You have always done so much for me and loved me so unconditionally. But I know it has not always been easy for you, working all the jobs that you do. Moving us here, away from our family and our Hispanic heritage, I know you struggle sometimes with the church and feeling like we don't belong because of who we are. And I never want to do anything that will make this life harder for you. And I don't want you to worry about me.

But I also want to be honest with you. I want you always to be a part of my life, even parts of it you won't fully get or understand. And I struggle to let you in because I worry you might stop loving me and that you might never want to talk to me again.

But here goes nothing. I'm gay. It is a part of who I am, and it is not going away. I have been praying about it for a long time, and I have asked God to take away the feelings. But I know now that whenever I ask God to change me, his response is he made me exactly how he wants me to be.

I also want you to know that I know you always wanted me to date a Christian, and I am. He loves God just as much as me, and he helps me feel closer to God. I know I love him, and he loves me, and God loves us, and God made us for each other.

The best part is that you already know him and love him. My boyfriend is Jason from church. Please know we are both the exact same people you knew before this letter. We just wanted you to know about us, and we have been praying for the day when you would find out. We have been praying you will still love us just like you always have. We have been praying that you will accept us as we are.

Love always,

Mario.

Session #22

Hey Aaron,

You probably heard the news. My little hometown is currently in the middle of this heated controversy about trying to remove any queer-related content from the local public library. It is just ridiculous. We queers pay taxes, too; we deserve to have access to some books or television shows or movies that represent us.

It is not like our library had much queer content anyway. I used to play a game, sometimes with Mario, where we could see how much openly queer-related content we could find in the library. Usually, we tied: zero to zero. It's hard to win a point for finding queer books when there are none. Mario often drove all the way to Big Rapids' library. One time, I scored a point because I found a book with God in the title. At first, I thought the librarians must have assumed it was a Christian-friendly book. And, I mean, it was. It was a book about a gay teen trying to understand his identity as a gay Christian. But I wondered if the librarians knew it had queer content in it, and they sneaked this one book in without the homophobic town folks noticing. The secret superheroes, librarians, fighting the fight against heteronormativity one straight passing book at a time.

Of course, now the librarians were a little more open about including openly queer content; they were under attack. These unassuming people, who just wanted to help patrons find their books and maybe shush people who were a little too loud, were now evil boogeymen bent on corrupting the youth. Yeah, I'll never understand why books became so contentious. I may be able to reason something like "those who control what we read, control what we think," but even then, I feel like this is just some middle school spat: a stupid, petty, annoying, childish squabble.

But I did know the damage could be real and felt for all the queer folks, especially those in middle school and high school. People spewed grotesque hate. People attacked them and tried to make them feel lesser and unworthy. People cried just thinking their precious kid might turn out queer, implying that our identities are something to be mourned, not celebrated.

A few days ago, I saw on social media that the City Council decided to hold a town hall meeting, allegedly so people could voice their opinions about the proposed ban on queer content in the library. From all I was learning about politics, I imagined it was more an opportunity for them to try to show they cared about what we thought and try to justify their actions. I struggled to decide if I wanted to go. I knew the hateful words would feel like darts stabbing me right in the heart. I knew I'd get angry and feel stressed. I knew that those fighting for queer rights would be outnumbered. I imagined I would be one of the few people there advocating against censorship.

But I also knew someone needed to attend and advocate for what was right and just. Someone had to challenge the hate and the discriminatory viewpoints of people who would strip away our rights and ability to love freely. Someone needed to show the middle schoolers and high schoolers they are loved. Folks care for them. What if Mario and I had that? How much better would our lives have been?

I knew this was about more than books. Yes, the books mattered. But the books represented our ability to be in the community. If they wanted to banish all the books that represented us, they would get rid of us all.

I recently attended a lecture at school about the 1960s civil rights movement. There, I learned about this amazing civil rights advocate, Ella Baker. She wrote about why seemingly small things matter so much, saying the sit-ins at restaurant counters were about much more than the burger. It was about dignity, freedom, and equality. Having books about you in the library isn't only about being able to read books. It's about whether you are viewed and treated as fully human.

I intended to get my books and eat burgers while reading them.

I went to the City Council meeting.

I approached City Hall slowly. I'd written a speech, but I hadn't decided if I wanted to deliver it. I was practicing my breathing techniques: breathe in slowly for four counts, hold my breath for four counts, exhale for four counts, hold again for four counts, and repeat. As I began to feel better, I looked around at the people who were also walking there. To my surprise, I saw an older, heterosexual couple. I assumed they were heterosexual at least. They both wore rainbow shirts and marched resolutely toward City Hall. Their determination resonated with every step. Their confidence boosted mine, and I began to pick up the pace. A slight smile appeared on my face as I nodded their way. They nodded back to me.

We arrived at the door at the same time. Taking another look at their shirts, I quickly exclaimed, "Hi! Thank you for coming."

Surprised with myself, I smiled and opened the door for them. The man simply responded, "Of course! We wouldn't miss this. It is long past time I gave the mayor a piece of my mind."

The anger and hurt in his voice shocked me. It felt like this man, with a little curve in his back and his white hair, might burst at any moment. As they walked through the door, the man went head to a table labeled, "Check in here." As he did, the woman said, "Thank you for holding the door. Would you like to sit with us?"

Maybe she could sense my nervousness as I sensed his anger and hurt?

"Yes, that would be wonderful," I answered.

"Great! My name's Gloria," She continued.

"Jason," I said, reaching out an arm towards hers, "Nice to meet you."

"Nice to meet you too," she turned and called toward her husband. "Herald, this is Jason. He is going to sit with us."

He turned and looked at me, "Nice to meet you, Jason. Do you want to sign up to speak? I am!"

Something about being with Gloria and Herald gave me the confidence boost I needed; I decided to give it a go. I replied, "Yes, I think I will."

After we signed in and signed up to speak, we took seats near the front of the City Council chambers and waited for the proceedings to start.

As you might expect, the City Council members all waxed poetically, or at least tried to wax poetically, about the importance of public discussion, consensus building, and listening to the voices of the people. Normally, I agreed, but the last part suddenly had me worried. If they listened to the voices of the people and the majority wanted to eliminate queer rights, then the minority, me, would have no protection or representation. Majority rules, it seemed to me, meant discrimination for the minority.

Want to take a guess at how many of the speakers quoted scripture to condemn homosexuality—their chosen term? The first few certainly did. They praised the traditional family values of the town. They praised the City Council for supporting Christians when Christians across the nation were under attack by the immoral gay rights movement. Funny, I do not recall any queer folks trying to get Bibles banned from local libraries. You can still find a Bible in most hotel rooms.

One brave soul advocated for creating a warm and inviting community, which meant the town should affirm and accept LGBTQ+ people—her words. I emphasize that because the earlier speakers used a wide array of terminology: homosexuality, sexual preference, sexual deviant, LGBTQ+, gay, and queer—in a way that showed the speaker probably still thought it was a slur. Maybe it still is?

I mention this because all the different terms people used really highlighted the unease of this topic. People didn't even really know how to talk about sexuality or gender identity, and yet here we were debating it.

After about seven speakers, the mayor called Herald's name. Energy radiated from Herald as he jumped from his seat and began the short walk over to the podium. He marched resolutely. I had not thought to ask before, but I immediately wondered if he served in the military. I didn't need to wait long to learn that he had.

Herald's speech went something like this:

I would say good evening to everyone, but tonight is not a very good evening. It is a sad evening and a heartbreaking evening. But I understand why it is happening. I do. I used to be like so many people in this room with my thinking about queer people. Raised in the church, I thought same-sex relationships were sinful. I really did. I was so stupid then. That was before I started studying the issue.

That was before my granddaughter came out to us. I'm here for her tonight. I'm here to say these continued attacks against queer people are discrimination, and the God I know is looking at this City Council with disgust. It is disgusting what you are doing tonight. It is disgusting that we have had to sit and listen to such hateful testimony. It's the hate in this room that makes it so people like my granddaughter move out of our town as soon as they can. Banning books isn't pro-family; it rips families apart.

Every year, when I march in the Veteran's Day parade, you all thank me for my service and my sacrifice. But who did I sacrifice for?

Looking back on it, I fought for a few things. Yes, I fought for folks' right to spew hateful garbage, as has been demonstrated tonight. But I also was fighting for the right of everyone to pursue their happiness. I was fighting for their right to express themselves in the way they wanted to do so.

Then, the mayor gave a fake little cough into the microphone, and eyes turned to him. The mayor said, void of any emotion, "We ask everyone to remain respectful. This is a difficult topic for us all."

I thought, okay, so reading scripture to imply that people in the room should go to hell is not disrespectful, but calling it all nonsense garbage is? Noted.

Flustered a bit, Herald continued, "I'm trying Mister Mayor. But, given what we are discussing, I would say I've been rather restrained." He returned to his speech.

I'll conclude by saying this. I did not fight for a town that continues to attack its children until they want to kill themselves. No, I did not. I encourage you all to support our queer friends and family members and oppose this ban.

To my surprise, about half of the room erupted into cheers and applause. Many more than I would have thought, given the previous... umm... testimonies. The mayor banged his gavel to quiet the room.

"Thank you," the mayor said flatly. Herald started walking back to his seat. One of the council women off to the left looked like she was sleeping. My blood had started boiling when they called my name.

Session #23

ERALD APPROACHED WHERE WE were sitting, mouthing something like "go get 'em" to me. I mouthed back, "Thank you."

My time had arrived. It was time for me to channel my hurt and frustration into a powerful message, and I hoped the City Council would side with me and with queer rights.

As I approached the podium, the mayor said something to the effect of, "Welcome." His flat tone really emphasized to me that we likely were not welcome, and they really wanted to pass this proposal without comment or controversy.

The words left my lips like I was in cruise control:

A couple of years ago, I survived the school shooting. Then, many in this community reached out to support us, the survivors. You said you loved us and cared about us and wanted us to have a better future. Even then, I knew the promise—the promise of love—was conditional. You would only love us if we fit your standards, and this proposal demonstrates that. This proposal shows you only care for and love certain members of the community. What you are doing is attacking queer people like me, who just want to live our lives.

The words just slipped out. I had not planned on adding the "like me" to the speech; it just happened. At that point in my speech, it felt like I was a video game character, and someone else had the controller. The "like me" happened automatically. In fact, for much of the speech, I felt like I was watching myself. I couldn't believe I was delivering this speech in front of... people, much less the City Council. But I knew I could not go back now, so I continued.

You do realize queer students died that day, don't you? The community didn't pull the trigger, but it did and still does cause harm.

Studies continually show that the mere introduction of anti-queer proposals and legislation causes stress, anxiety, depression, and suicidal ideation in the LGBTQ+ community. Banning these books will show to many people living here in Small Rapids that they do not belong. Why do you think so many young people are moving away? Why do you think so many young people refuse to attend church? It is because they are sick of the "unconditional" love, of the judgment, or the thinly veiled contempt and hate. This policy is short-sighted and stifles free expression. Remember the golden rule. Do unto others as you would have them do unto you. I know many in this room do not want devotionals and Bibles taken out of the library. Do not set the precedent that political trends determine what we can and cannot access. Next time, you might not like what is banned.

I finished my speech to cheers, at least from about half of the crowd. I simultaneously felt proud and disappointed in myself. Proud because I'd done it; I had stood up and advocated for myself. Disappointed because I wish I'd done better. I felt a little unfocused when giving the speech. I wish I had done more to prepare what I wanted to say. As I walked back to my seat, I felt nervous. What had I done? I outed myself, and I was not sure it would matter.

As I returned to my seats, both Herald and Gloria mouthed, "Great job" to me. Their smiles kindled a warm feeling in my chest and stomach. But my mind still raced, wondering if my speech made a difference.

Of course, several homophobic speeches followed mine, continuing the harmful practices I had just critiqued. My mind wandered from feelings of anger, frustration, hopelessness, and self-doubt. Could anyone ever craft an argument that would persuade these people?

Finally, the mayor called another speaker, David Williams. I hadn't seen him since the march against gun violence. Just then, several thoughts simultaneously jumped into my mind. I hoped he was about to bring the fire and deliver a speech to move this conversation forward. I wondered if he would affirm queer rights. Surely, he would, given that he supported gun control measures, right? I also wanted to ask him if he was queer too. Suddenly, it dawned on me; I had just come out to someone from high school.

I did not have to wait long to know what David thought about the issue. He started,

I am so utterly disappointed that you all have gathered us here tonight to listen to all this bigoted nonsense about queer people. It is just so sad, but I know the real reason you are doing this.

As I was preparing for tonight, I remembered some of you tried to defund the library a few years ago, basically under the cover of night. When I realized attacks on the library were not new, I started to investigate why some of you would go after the library.

I checked out your campaign's financial reports, and there was the answer. These financial reports are publicly available, and anyone can access them on the web. In fact, they can even use the computers at the library to read them.

You've received maximum donations from several prominent companies that sell books, films, internet services, and other services provided for free by our library. That's what this is about: finding a wedge issue so you can defund the library and get more campaign donations. This is about

appeasing your donors, and sadly you are willing to cause so much harm to do that.

The mayor loudly banged his gavel and exclaimed, "David, you will respect the etiquette of this chamber. I have warned you before. Make sure you are being appropriate—"

David cut him off, "Etiquette? Appropriate? You just let people spew violent and hateful words. You haven't acted appropriately. How dare you tell us to respect you and your rules!"

"I am going to have to ask you to leave," the mayor said. "You are clearly not mature enough to handle this conversation in a civil manner."

"You have an awful and twisted understanding of civility," David spat back. "You are the one who lacks civility and decorum."

"Don't make me have the officers put you in handcuffs," the mayor continued.

"Fine, I'll leave. And I hope those donations keep you warm at night," David said rather coolly and walked out of the chamber. That got the crowd going. Several cheers erupted. Gasps echoed from behind me.

"Ladies and Gentlemen, we welcome public discussion about what content the library should offer, but we cannot accept personal attacks and rebukes of the motives of the council," the mayor stated, his effort to suppress agitation clear in his voice. Several people booed.

Another bang of the gavel sounded, and the mayor announced, "This meeting is adjourned."

Another round of gasps and jeers followed the mayor and the rest of the council members as they filled out of the room. And, just like that, it was over. David had certainly made an impression, and I smiled. At least no one else would spew toxic vomit out of their mouths tonight.

"Well, I don't think the City Council liked hearing the truth," Gloria sighed as she started to stand up.

"Yeah, I guess not," I said, a little stunned they just left like that. They did not even try to respond to the accusations of corruption.

"David sure knows out to stir up the crowd; it is all that speech and debate training, I bet," Herald nodded along.

"Yeah, I knew him in high school," I said.

"Ah, yes, I remember he was in the school shooting, too; I'm so sorry to hear you had to go through it, too," Herald continued as Gloria reached over and patted me on the shoulder.

"I'm sorry too, Jason. Your speech was powerful, very moving," Gloria said.

"Thank you, I wished I had practiced it a bit more," I responded hesitantly.

"I think your speech was spot on," Herald said.

"Thanks, I appreciate it. I liked your speech too," I stated.

"Say Jason, do you have people who can talk to about all of this? The book ban, sexuality, religion, all of that?" Gloria asked.

I thought for a moment, and I really didn't. I have been holding it all inside ever since I lost Mario. So, I uttered tentatively, "Nope, not really."

"Well then, I want to invite you to a small group meeting we have about queer rights, Christianity, and a bunch of other related topics," Gloria exclaimed.

"Oh? Yeah, that sounds nice," I said.

"Yeah, it is nice to have community," Herald confirmed, "It is every other Wednesday night at Central Street United Methodist Church. It's in the big city. It is a bit of a hike for us, but we wouldn't miss it. We usually go to church there, too."

"Central Street United Methodist Church?" I replied, recalling a warm hug with a fiery red-haired pastor.

"Yeah, it is a mouthful; I have a card with my contact information. Reach out for the details," Herald said.

"Thanks, I actually think I've heard of the church before," I said. "I think I'll attend."

"Well, it was nice to meet you, Jason," Gloria exclaimed, "I hope to see you there."

Session #24

H I Aaron,

Wednesday night, I found myself driving to my queer-affirming meeting at Central Street United Methodist Church.

Herald texted me all the information I needed to find it, but it was hard to miss. The large, red-bricked building loomed large over the neighboring houses. With white trim and a tall steeple, you could see the building long before you arrived.

I found a parking space about a block away. As I approached, I noticed the large rainbow banner hanging near the front door. Its sign read, "Central Street United Methodist Church: All Are Welcome!" My heart skipped a beat, and I tried to think if I had ever seen a church that was so visibly pro-queer. Sadly, I could not. My heart suddenly started yearning for this church, and I wanted to be a part of it.

I reached the door. After a deep breath, I reached out, turned the handle, and entered.

The church looked huge from the outside, but the entryway was rather cozy. The lights were bright enough to see everything but dim enough to ensure my eyes did not feel like they were being burned out. There was a lovely scent in the air. I couldn't identify it, but it was comforting. Maybe something like frankincense and lavender? Peppermint, too, perhaps?

And there, the pastor with red hair stood. Before I could really process everything, I heard a loud and enthusiastic, "Welcome! I heard we might have a new visitor today!"

I made eye contact with her and rather shyly said, "Hi! Yeah, that's me."

"Well, welcome to Central Street," she continued. "I'm Pastor Esther, and I'm so happy you are here."

"I'm excited to be here too; I actually remember you from Pride a few years ago, I think," I replied.

"Oh? That might have been me. We try to get to Pride as often as we can; I love that our church can have a presence there," Pastor Esther exclaimed. "And, just so you know, we will be meeting in the classroom off to the right."

"Okay, thank you!" I responded as I excitedly walked off to the room, although I must admit I had a few nervous butterflies flying around in my stomach.

I could instantly tell the room was also used for children's Sunday school. A massive mural of Noah and the Ark plastered the far wall. The pairs of giraffes, elephants, and lions all looked like they were smiling as they entered the massive wooden boat. A few toys lined the walls, but in the middle of the room, white plastic desks were clustered together to form a rectangle with enough seats for about a dozen or so people.

I recognized two faces immediately. Gloria and Herald were sitting next to each other and adjacent to a Black woman with naturally curly hair. As soon as I realized they were there, I heard my name. "Jason, welcome!"

It was Herald's, closely followed by Gloria's: "I am so glad you could make it!"

"I'm excited to be here," I said as I walked over to them.

"Jason, is it? Nice to have you here," the Black woman exclaimed, reaching out her hand to shake mine.

"Yes, Jason, thanks for having me," I replied.

"Of course! We love to have new faces. My name's Cathy, Cathy Smith," she said.

A commotion sounded in the entryway, and within seconds, several more people arrived. To be honest, at this point, I was feeling a bit overwhelmed. I remembered some of the breathing techniques, so I moved to one side and focused on breathing in for a few seconds, holding my breath, and breathing out. I didn't really have a reason to feel nervous or anxious; I sort of felt like I needed to make a good first impression. I wanted to remember all their names, but I struggled with the barrage of names and faces. I was already feeling anxious and embarrassed for *maybe* needing to ask them their names again.

I think there was a Randy and a Jude. I certainly missed the name of one of the adults, a gentleman wearing a Target uniform. The one person who was unmistakable was, I assume, a teenager, probably a freshman or sophomore in high school. She had bright pink hair, and a massive smile illuminated the rest of her face. Her smile reminded me of Mario.

"Hey everyone," Cathy exclaimed, "how are you all doing?"

She was met with a chorus of positive comments in return.

One lady, a Black woman with a good amount of steel in her hair, beelined over to me. I instantly recognized her as the woman who prayed for Mario and me. She reached out her hand and carefully clasped my hand in hers. She said, "My name's Ruth."

"I'm Jason. Nice to meet you!" I replied. I will say one thing: this group of people welcomed me in such a warm and caring manner. I was beginning to feel like I belonged, like I finally had a community where I could just be myself: queer and Christian. "I think you prayed for me at Pride a few years ago."

"Oh, that could have been me!" Ruth exclaimed. "I love going to Pride and praying for folks. You can just feel the love in the air."

"Yes, exactly right," I said. "It's beautiful to see."

"It is. Well, I am so happy you're here," Ruth said, "I have learned so much from this group; it has been such a wonderful experience for me, and I hope it is for you too."

"I have a feeling it will be," I replied.

"Okay, everyone, I think we can go ahead and get started," Pastor Esther exclaimed as everyone started finding seats. The all-too-familiar mixture of nervousness and excitement continued to flood my body, and I could barely contain myself. Have you ever started watching a movie and you just know that it will be wonderful, and you are looking forward to every moment, cherishing every image and line? Even before you'd watched much of it, you'd already decided you never wanted it to end. No? Well, I have. It was exactly how I felt. Somehow, I knew this would be the start of the next chapter of my life, and I couldn't wait for it.

"Do we want to start with a quick prayer?" Pastor Esther asked.

Several head nods showed affirmation, and Ruth offered, "I'm happy to lead it, Pastor."

"Thank you, Ms. Ruth," Pastor Esther said as she folded her hands and closed her eyes. I followed suit.

"God, we thank you for yet another day where we can breathe the air and feel the sun's rays on us. We thank you once again for bringing us together to have important conversations about how we can best do your will. We also thank you for bringing us a new face, Jason, and we pray our time is a blessing to him," Ruth started.

"Amen!" Cathy interjected.

"We also pray, Lord, that we use our time wisely and that we learn how to show your love and serve every one of your children, especially your LGBTQ+ children. In Jesus' name we pray, amen," Ruth said.

A series of other amens, including mine, followed. My eyes opened, and I felt even more ready for what was about to happen.

"Well, friends, I'm so curious! Where did the Holy Spirit bring you this week?" Pastor Esther asked with renewed joy and excitement on her face.

"The Holy Spirit took us to the City Council meeting about banning books, and we got to meet Jason. And what a blessing. The meeting itself was heartbreaking, but I am happy we were able to connect," Herald started.

"Ah, I thought as much! Unfortunately, I couldn't make it. There was a scheduling conflict with the United in Struggle meeting about criminal justice reform," Cathy exclaimed.

"It is both a blessing and a source of deep sadness that there's so much justice work happening," Pastor Esther stated, the joy on her face replaced with something more resonant of an emotional void. "Thank you all for your commitment to building a more just world."

"Yeah, and unfortunately, I was also... unable to go to the book-banning meeting. I had to work and would not have been able to get transportation," the man in the Target uniform said. His words were deliberate but also quite labored. It seemed like he needed to take deep breaths to keep speaking.

"I have my driver's license now, Shawn, just text me!" The young woman with pink hair interjected.

"Thanks for the offer, Naomi... but," Shawn began.

Naomi interrupted, "We should all get there if we can. I just couldn't go."

The man sitting next to Naomi shot her a look, and said, "Her dad made her finish her homework instead. But, seriously, Shawn, we would be happy to take you next time." He was evidently the dad in question, Jude.

"Okay... I just don't think I would ever want to say anything," Shawn continued.

"I think just being there is important," Gloria stated, "I didn't say anything. But I might want to give our mayor a piece of my mind next time."

"That will be a sight to behold," Herald joked.

"Well, tell us about it all then. Tell us all about the City Council meeting. Then I can fill you in on the United in Struggle meeting," Cathy got everyone back on track, turning to look at me, Gloria, and Herald.

Herald jumped right in, "As you can imagine, it was quite a disappointment. The City Council basically stormed off! But it was heartening to see so many people speak in support of the queer community."

"Certainly, more people spoke against the ban than would have even five years ago," Gloria agreed.

My recollection was different. I didn't think many spoke against the ban, but I guess it is easier to remember the awfully terrible, mean-spirited, and just plain cringy speeches. It was like Ruth read my mind because she quickly stated, "Yeah, but the whole situation is still so difficult for people to handle. Sometimes, it is hard to think of any of this as progress. How long must we wait until people start treating others like people?"

The words left my lips automatically, "It is hard for me to be honest. I keep going from feeling hopeful, to feeling like it all is false hope, and feeling totally depressed."

Cathy concurred, "It's the same with me and my racial justice work. But I believe God is calling me to work towards justice, even when I'm not sure I'm making any impact."

"There was one speech that made my day, though. One of the guys I went to high school with gave this speech about how the City Council is attacking the library to support big businesses. I loved how he just called out their motives. I thought he was courageous," I continued with a little smirk emerging on my face.

"David's speech was just amazing," Herald uttered as I finished.

"Our David? The one who attends this church?" Pastor Esther asked.

"Yeah, our David gave just a wonderful speech calling out their corruption," Gloria responded. My heart jumped. Did David attend this group? The anxious butterflies started swarming in my stomach. The balance between anxiety and excitement suddenly tilted toward nervousness.

"And you went to high school with him, Jason? What a small world," Pastor Esther continued.

"Yeah, we went to high school together," I replied.

"Oh, child! So, you experienced the shooting too?" Ruth suddenly asked.

My heart stung, and I lowered my head, but I answered, "Yeah, I was there."

A moment of silence followed before Pastor Esther said calmly, slowly, and clearly, "Healing from such trauma is hard. I believe Christ calls us to be in community with each other so we can help each other through our trauma and the pain of the world. I know I can speak for everyone when I say we will all be praying for you."

"Yes, we will. I will pray for you," Ruth nodded.

"Speaking of David, I'm surprised he is not here," Cathy redirected the conversation, and I gave her a relieved smile.

"He told me that, unfortunately, he… was not going to be able to make it tonight," Shawn chimed in.

"Too bad. I wonder what he thinks about the whole 'ban the books' situation," said a man with white hair and a suit jacket. He had a little rainbow pin on his lapel. I later learned his name was Randy Lowe.

"And I need to talk to him about the next potential issue for United in Struggle. Rumor says some legislators at the state level want to propose a new private prison," Cathy explained.

"Really?" Ruth's voice rose in volume.

"Unfortunately, yes," Cathy answered. "It might happen quickly, so we need to stay on our toes."

"Let us know if we can do anything," Randy said.

"Hopefully, it doesn't come to that, but you all will know if it does," Cathy stated firmly.

Session #25

HI AARON,

My nightmares returned the other day. I haven't had them for a long time, and I'm concerned about why they have started haunting me again. My main nightmare hasn't changed; it's me reliving the shooting. Sometimes, the setting changes, but it always ends with me running away from the gunfire. The shots get louder and louder. I try to run faster and faster, but I'm struggling to breathe. I know I'm running out of steam; I simply can't keep sprinting as fast as I want to. The shots are right behind me, and I wake, gasping for breath.

Two nights ago, I had another one. I was with Mario, and we were about to watch this movie. Turns out, the movie was a horror flick. I am not a big fan of scary movies, not even as an excuse to snuggle with someone. He hadn't realized it was a hack-and-slash movie either. So, when Mario grabbed the remote to turn it off, we fell into the film, becoming a part of its plot.

Immediately, we saw a stabbing on the street corner; blood squirted everywhere. We didn't see the killer, but we knew they were hiding in the shadows. We turned and started to run. We ran and ran, but eventually, Mario turned toward me and said, "Keep going."

He stopped, but I kept running. Why did I keep running? I wanted to stop and tell him 'no'. But my legs keep moving. I begged my body to stop, but it refused. I heard the yells, the guttural screams. I jerked out of the dream and woke up in my bed. Safe and sound but drenched in sweat with my heart pounding. Out of breath, I needed to sleep to recover from my... sleep.

But I don't get why I'm having these nightmares now. I swear things have been getting better. Although maybe they aren't?

Take this week: Herald's letter to the editor was published in the local newspaper, and it was shared widely online. The letter was essentially a rehashing of what he had told the City Council. He emphasized how, as a veteran, he did not fight for some ambiguous notion of freedom that only applied to straight couples, like him and Gloria. It has simply been wonderful to know people who are fighting the fight, if you will.

Of course, people write the cruelest things online. And it was easy to find a plethora of homophobic comments about his article. A small part of me wanted to engage, but another part of me knew it was futile. After all this time, how did all the homophobias still get to me? I thought I was stronger than that. I felt my body preparing me to fight and spend all day responding to the hate. Maybe my unconsciousness needed to vent after witnessing those hateful, cruel, and disparaging comments.

I hadn't been thinking about this advocacy work for long, maybe a few weeks, maybe less. I already felt like we were going through the motions. Someone would do or say something incredibly anti-queer. But their letters were published and circulated in the press. We expressed our rightful outrage at the ongoing harm being inflicted on us by an exclusionary society. Then, our or someone else's letter condemning the comment would make the rounds. Nothing happens. Then, we get attacked for being too sensitive. It often felt like they wanted us to react—as if they found some perverse joy in people expressing their pain.

The City Council had already scheduled another meeting so people could come and share their perspectives on the "gay issue" the city was facing. I knew I would attend. And I knew Gloria and Herald were going, too. Pastor Esther said she would try to make it. I thought about giving another speech. Herald would. We planned to express our sadness, frustration, and anger. We would articulate clear arguments about why inclusion matters. But it wouldn't matter. We knew, deep down, nothing would change.

I arrived at Central Street the Sunday after the small group meeting. Ruth and Cathy invited me to attend just as we were finishing our discussion on Wednesday. I didn't hesitate. I knew attending this church with these people was the best decision for me. I desperately wanted to be in a community with people who affirmed and supported my right to exist; I also wanted to use my life to make the world a better place for all.

I entered the venue and immediately saw Cathy, who turned and waved at me.

"Welcome, Jason!" Cathy exclaimed.

I waved and, a little more quietly, muttered, "Hi, Cathy."

"How are you?" she asked. Before I had a chance to respond, she was grabbing folks to introduce them to me.

What followed was a blur. I met so many new people and "learned" so many new names. And the family dynamics! I doubted I would ever figure out who was married to whom and which children went with which parents. But despite the overwhelm, the atmosphere still felt warm. The smiles on their faces and the buzz of chit-chat confirmed this was still the right place for me.

Fortunately, I arrived right before the service started, so I was saved by Pastor Esther and others telling folks to move into the sanctuary. I sat with Cathy and readied myself for worship, excited to experience a service unlike any other.

The service was simply beautiful.

We started by singing an old favorite of mine, but the meaning really struck home. So many Christian hymns seem selfish. I admit I know it is important to thank God for sending Jesus to save us from our sins. At least, I understand it logically, but I am not sure I ever really feel it. Because most of these songs just repeat how we are saved. God saved *us*. *We* have been freed from sin. *We* have been blessed. Jesus died for *us*.

Over and over again, the songs only talk about what we, Christians, get in exchange for believing. Our relationship with God is reduced to an essentially transactional one. We believe in God, and in return, God rewards us with salvation. It is purely economic: a rational decision calculus. God gets praise in exchange for saving us from our sins.

Faith seemed like nothing more than a business transaction.

The feeling never sat well with me. I always felt like being a Christian meant I was in a relationship with God; it felt much more meaningful.

But this song was different. It wasn't purely in the past tense like many contemporary Christian songs, praising God for what he has already done. Instead, this song was about our Christian values and our desire to serve others. The song asked others to join our efforts to show mercy, to pursue justice, and to love tenderly. The song placed Christianity, not in the past, with Christ's sacrifice, but in our ongoing pursuit of living Christ-like in the present and for a more just and inclusive future.

The song felt like the congregation's mission for justice. The raw beauty of singing about justice brought tears to my eyes. I've known hardship, and I wanted to become more acquainted with justice.

I needed a tissue during Pastor Esther's sermon; fortunately, Cathy had plenty. She needed a tissue, too.

Pastor Esther read from Matthew 25:

For I was hungry, and you gave me something to eat, I was thirsty, and you gave me something to drink, I was a stranger and you invited me in, I needed clothes and you clothed me, I was sick and you looked after me, I was in prison and you came to visit me. Then the righteous will answer him, 'Lord, when did we see you hungry and feed you, or thirsty and give you something to drink? When did we see you a stranger and invite you in, or needing clothes and clothe you? When did we see you sick or in prison and go to visit you?' Truly, I tell you, whatever you did for one of these least of these brothers and sisters of mine, you did for me.

Pastor Esther finished by saying, "The word of God, for the people of God."

Everyone, other than me, replied, "Thanks be to God!"

The church I grew up in never had people respond in that way, but I liked it. I liked how it helped me feel connected to everyone else in the congregation. Then, Pastor Esther linked the church's mission to serve the community to the passage she'd chosen. She was incredibly eloquent:

I feel so fortunate to serve a congregation that cares so much about showing their faith in public. Let me be clear. We do not just declare we are Christians and move on; we engage with the community and show God's love through our actions. I truly believe that. So many of you have talked to me about ways to support the temporarily unhoused folks in this city. Now, we are in the planning process for opening up a clothing ministry. 'For I needed clothes, and you clothed me.' Together, we are working to advise people about the criminal justice system.

After this service, folks will continue reading books about mass incarceration and our Christian duty to help those impacted by the system. Several of you plan to go to the Capital to advocate against another for-profit, private prison. 'I was in prison, and you came to visit me.' Many of you have been active in advocacy around healthcare and ensuring folks can get the help they need. 'I was sick, and you looked after me.'

Of course, we always find ourselves with more work to do. And I must pause about the ongoing controversies as it relates to our queer siblings in Christ.

It breaks my heart that the issue of same-sex relationships still fractures families and the church. Many of us, including myself, learned a particular way of reading scripture which condemned queer folks. I call on all of us to pray for congregations struggling with this issue, with families who have had someone come out as queer, and for the queer folks who face alienation for expressing themselves and how God created them.

The flags outside our church are a promise that we want to do better, a sign we believe God's table is open to everyone, and that we are here to affirm and cherish queer children of God.

Again, I am so thankful that I have this opportunity to serve the many 'least of these' in our community with you all.

Pastor Esther's sermon overwhelmed me, but in a good way. I had never experienced a pastor openly declare the church must serve and help queer folks. I found her sermon incredibly refreshing. I had finally found a Christian model that didn't openly condemn me; instead, it affirmed me—all of me.

But as is always the case, when something good happens, my memories of the past come rushing back. Good comes with a twinge of bittersweet. What if she had been the pastor we saw that night? The night another pastor declared homosexuality a sin, when I saw the pain in Mario's eyes for the first time. Would our lives have turned out differently?

The service ended, and people started gathering up their things and meandering over to the coffee station. Coffee sounded so good to me. I think I'm becoming addicted. Scratch that, I am addicted to coffee now. I used to need cream and sugar, but not anymore.

As I started sipping, Ruth came over to me and said, "I'm overjoyed you decided to come to church. We need more young folks like you who want to advocate for justice and inclusion."

"I'm glad I came, too. I've needed a church like this for a long time," I replied.

"It can be hard for us who have experienced so much pain because of our fellow Christians. It can be hard to forgive, but I know I love so much more deeply because of all of it," Ruth stated. "I hope this can be an answer to the prayer I said for you at Pride."

"I hope so, too," I said.

"I know you do. I can tell. You care deeply," Ruth continued. "And I'm glad you do. The work won't be finished in my lifetime, but I know we will continue to help bend the arc of history toward justice."

"Is that King?" I asked, referencing Martin Luther King.

"Yes, some of us are old enough to remember him when he was alive, you know?" Ruth continued.

"Surely, not you?" I said with a bit of a laugh.

"Maybe someday we can talk about it," Ruth chuckled. "But, for now, I'm violating doctor's orders and getting some cookies."

The next two conversations happened so quickly they merged into one another, becoming a blur.

As I was finishing pouring a cup of coffee, I noticed Cathy approaching. I turned and greeted her, "Hey Cathy, how are you?"

"To tell the truth, I've been better. I was wondering if you wanted to attend a criminal justice reform protest?" she asked. "One about the private prison?"

"They proposed it?" Ruth exclaimed.

"Yes, I think it happened late in the day on Friday," Cathy continued.

"Bet they hoped no one would notice," Ruth scoffed.

"Ummm... when's the protest?" I replied hesitantly. "I'd like to come."

"This coming Friday. We will probably need to leave the church parking lot at like eight in the morning," Cathy answered.

"Okay! That works! I don't have any classes on Friday," I exclaimed.

"Awesome! Looking forward to having you," she stated.

"I'm in, too," Ruth said.

"Good," Cathy replied.

After briefly meeting several other members of the congregation, whose names I had already forgotten, I started heading for the door, but I heard my name echoing through the crowd.

"Hey, Jason! Wait up!" David's voice rang out.

I turned to see him speed-walking towards me. He half waved, and I returned it. When he was close enough, I said, "Hey, David. Long time, no see."

"Yeah, it has been a minute," David exclaimed. "But I'm so glad to see you here."

"It is good to be here. I wanted to chat with you after the City Council meeting, but you made an epic exit," I laughed.

"I just wanted to rile them up a bit," he said, smiling mischievously.

"Well, you succeeded. That's for sure. It was great, and they needed to hear it," I told him.

"I heard you came to the conversations about Christianity and sexuality, or whatever we're calling the group." His reply was matter of fact. No hint of a sneer or slur.

"Oh, yes, I did. It was wonderful. It felt wonderful," I said, hearing my voice trail off at the end.

"Hey, sometimes Ruth and I get together to talk about current events, race, sexuality, and our faith. Would you like to join us?" he asked. "We usually meet at this place called the Common Grounds."

"Oh, the coffee place that's sort of along the highway back home?" I asked. "The one with the massive wood carved coffee bean near the entrance?"

"Yeah, that one," he confirmed. "They have like soup and sandwiches and snacks too."

"I'd love to," I replied. "I'd love to support any and all affirming company right now."

"Okay!" he said, "Let me get your number."

Session #26

HI AARON,

On Wednesday morning, I arrived at Common Grounds. I was a bit early, and the parking lot seemed busy. So, I decided to race in and make sure I found a spot for me, David, and Ruth. Despite the vast number of folks in the coffee shop, the atmosphere was strangely calming. Luckily for us, most people were grabbing coffee and leaving. It wasn't hard to find a table where the three of us could fit.

Eventually, Ruth and David joined me. David got water and a ginger-molasses cookie, reminding me of Mario's sweet tooth. *Did he like the cinnamon rolls at the Golden Skillet too?* Ruth went with a dark roast coffee, basically the opposite of any coffee I've ever tasted. The strong aroma reached me know, and I winced a bit as I thought about what it must taste like. *Maybe someday I could drink something so strong, but not today.* The conversation turned serious quickly.

"Can I ask you a sort of invasive question, Jason?" Ruth asked. "You don't have to answer if you don't want to."

"Ummm... sure," I responded positively, although her question worried me.

"Why are you interested in attending the private prison protest? Are you interested in other racial justice protests or just that one?" Ruth questioned.

I was stumped and needed a moment to think. When Cathy asked if I wanted to attend the protest, I instantly said yes. I didn't put a lot of thought into it; I think I simply wanted to spend time with them. To be with other like-minded folks.

I answered Ruth hesitantly, "Honestly, I think it was as simple as wanting to spend time with you all. I want to learn more about advocacy and how my faith connects to it. I have a deep desire to push for a more perfect world for all, and I thought this could be a start."

Ruth chuckled as she nodded at me. "Well, I think you've come to the right place. Most of my friends nowadays do a lot of service and racial justice work. We spend our retirement making the world better for the next generation. At least, that's what we tell ourselves. I know Cathy considers this her life's work."

I continued, "I know I have a lot to learn, especially about race and racism. But I do want to learn more. Be an ally, you know."

"I've learned a lot by just shutting up and listening," David interjected.

"Just like I, an elderly, Black, straight woman, have learned so much about sexuality by listening," Ruth agreed. "I'm curious. Why do you want to learn more about racism? I don't want you to feel pressure or anything."

I was in the middle of a sip of my latte, giving me a moment to pause.

"I haven't met too many young White folks really interested in it and wanting to do something about it. So, I'm really just curious," Ruth continued.

I took a deep breath. I knew my answer, but did I want to share it? Was it the right answer? Would I convey my feelings in the way I wanted to? A part of me sensed Ruth already knew. She knew I had something buried inside that motivated me—something making me want to learn more.

I raised a fingertip to the corner of my eye as I started, "Honest is the best policy, right? It is a long story, I guess. Please forgive me if I start crying."

"Cry all you want. I have tissues," Ruth stated.

David simply nodded. I wonder if he knew where this was headed.

"I know I mentioned the shooting to you," I said. "The one that David and I survived."

"Yes," Ruth confirmed, and David let out a loud exhale. I knew the exhale well; it was the heartbreak from thinking about the horrific day trying to force its way out.

"Well, I lost someone that day. He's the one who really taught me about race and racism," I quickly sputtered. I just needed to get it all out, I told myself. It was just like jumping into the deep end of a pool or ripping off a band-aid: a moment of fear and pain followed by relief.

After a moment's pause, David simply asked, "Mario?"

"Yeah, Mario," I responded.

After another moment of silence, Ruth slowly asked, "Mario?"

"Mario was a star athlete, but he was also so kind and caring. He and Jason were basically inseparable from what I remember," David responded enthusiastically at first but then trailed off at the end. I could barely hear him when he said, "Remember." I wondered if that's what an epiphany sounded like.

"He was actually the guy who was with me when you prayed for us at pride, Ruth," I stated as calmly as I could. "He was Hispanic. And I say Hispanic because that's what he always called himself. I know other people nowadays might say Latino or Latinx. Anyway, there was this one time we were together, and some folks yelled slurs at him from a passing car. The pain in his face was unbearable. I knew in an instant the slur created a wound, but I had no idea what to do. My mind went blank."

I paused again for a moment before continuing, "You know, Ruth, I could probably give a lot of reasons and examples about why I want to learn more about race and racism, but it all comes back to that at the end of the day: Mario and my love for him."

Silence overtook the conversation again. I felt my heart beating more quickly. Doubt found its way into my thoughts as I wondered if I'd said too much. Fortunately, Ruth eventually said, "Thank you for sharing, Jason. And I'm so sorry for your loss."

"Thanks," I said. "And what I really want to say is I want to be an advocate because I love people; I want to help make the world a better place for them... us. I know there are so many other Marios out there. People who experience racial injustice and hate. People who feel they don't belong—or can't belong—because they are queer, or because of their skin tone, or because of their gender, or because they weren't born wealthy, or because they have a disability. Or people who can't afford the opportunities the rest of us have had. People who die due to gun violence."

"It all comes from a place of love," Ruth murmured.

"Yes, all the hurt is because I love," I agreed. "And I want to make things better so those I love don't need to feel the pain I feel."

"I suppose I should share how I came to want to learn more about sexuality," Ruth responded. "Especially since some people seem to believe us older Black folk only vote against queer rights."

"They do say that, don't they," David agreed.

"They do?" I asked.

"Sadly, some do. And it's nonsense. Most of us oppressed folks know we need to stick together. But I must admit that my thoughts about sexuality changed a lot—quite a long time ago. I never really despised people who were gay, and I always thought I should show them love. But maybe I didn't really understand why promoting queer rights mattered for me as a Black, straight woman. I didn't know anyone at the time, at least I didn't know if I knew, if that makes sense. I imagine a lot more people were in the closet in those days. But it was Bayard Rustin who really changed the way I thought about sexuality," Ruth stated.

"Who?" I asked.

"Oh, Bayard Rustin. It is so sad, so few people know about him. What do they teach you in school anyway? Rustin was Dr. King's left-hand man, so to speak. At least, that is how I remember it. He planned the March on Washington, where King gave his 'I Have a Dream' speech. We would not have King's 'Dream' if it were not for Rustin. A gay, Black civil rights advocate," Ruth responded.

"Oh? I had no idea. I've never heard anything about him," I said, my mind already spinning with this new information about the civil rights movement.

"Definitely research him if you get a chance," Ruth responded. "He is one of the many folks they don't teach about in school, but they definitely should."

"Yeah, I'll look him up," I promised.

I left the meeting excited. I wanted to learn more about Bayard Rustin, and I was so happy that I could continue learning more about sexuality, race, religion, and social movements. I also felt a strange sense of comfort in having told them about Mario. Although, for a few moments, I felt like I had betrayed his trust. He never gave me permission to share his story with others, but I needed to figure out a way to tell my story. And, as you can tell, he is a key part of it. I think he would be okay with me sharing, especially if he knew it could help me.

Session #27

H¹ ᴀᴀʀᴏɴ,

We arrived at the Capitol Building on Friday morning around 9:45 am. David drove Ruth, Cathy, and me. When we arrived, a group had already gathered on the front lawn. The massive white dome of the Capitol Rotunda loomed large in the background. News crews had set up their tripods as more and more people gathered. I prayed none of the reporters asked to interview me.

I started noticing the signs: "Criminal Justice Reform Now!," "No Private Prisons!," "No School to Prison Pipeline!," and "Legalize Weed!"

The words burst through my lips, "I wonder why people have signs about legalizing pot."

Oh, my naivety. David looked at me and kindly said, "Well, I think people are concerned that so many Black and Brown folks keep getting locked up for something that's legal in other states."

"Yeah, I bet they are trying to build more jails to hold more and more Black folks," Ruth muttered grimly.

"Oh, I hadn't thought of it that way," I replied.

"But it is tricky. So many issues are interconnected, it can be hard to stay on message," Cathy exclaimed. "And I bet making this about weed will get more people on board, but it will probably alienate others."

"So much complexity around what seems like such a simple issue," I stated.

"That's why the political communication consultants and strategists stay in business," David joked.

"Well, I'm planning on keeping it simple today. 'Stop locking Black and Brown people up for something White folks are making millions off of elsewhere,'" Ruth stated.

She sighed and finished her thought, "Sadly, it doesn't really have a nice ring to it."

"Yeah, it's a tad hard to chant," Cathy agreed. "Although, it is so true."

"We might just have to use the no justice, no peace chant," David said.

"I hope they have some other ones," Cathy exclaimed.

A moment later, we reached the rest of the crowd. And we arrived just in time.

Someone, who I assumed was the protest's organizer, started yelling instructions with a bullhorn. He exclaimed, "Folks, we are going to start heading into the Capitol. The plan is to meet in the east side hearing room on the second floor. We ask you to let those who need to use the elevators use them first. If you can use the stairs, please do so."

He paused for a moment as another person whispered something into his ear. He continued, "Okay, y'all. We have been informed we cannot take any signs into the Capitol Building which use rulers, sticks, or wood, I guess of any kind to hold up the sign. Apparently, there is a concern people could use them as a weapon."

"Really? A sign is a weapon?" The words just left my mouth.

"Right?!" David responded.

The guy with the bullhorn said, "So, you can just leave them by the entrance as we proceed into the building. Alright! Let's go advocate for justice."

What had felt like an ominous silence moments before—the calm before the storm—burst into a frenzy of movement. The potential energy turned kinetic.

To Cathy's delight, protesters started chanting, "Hey, hey, ho, ho, private prisons gotta go!"

Cathy yelled as loud as she could, and I joined her.

As we started moving, Ruth said, "Y'all, I'm probably going to need to use the elevator, but you all can go ahead without me."

"You sure?" Cathy asked.

"Yeah, I want you all to get good seats," Ruth responded.

Good seats we did not get. The hearing room was already packed, and folks were congregating in the rotunda right outside the door. I paused for a moment, reflecting on where I had found myself. A few weeks ago, I would never have imagined I would be here in the Capitol's dome. The rotunda was simply gorgeous. It was sad to think such concerning legislation had been passed here. As I looked up toward the top of the majestic dome, I felt something. I can only describe it as a divine presence. God was with us. It was a warm embrace telling me I was doing exactly what I needed to be doing. A deep breath calmed my nerves. I hadn't really noticed how tense I was feeling until I looked up toward the top of the rotunda—toward Heaven. But once I did, my muscles relaxed. My stomach unclenched.

"I guess it is a good thing so many people are here," Cathy said.

"Definitely a good thing," David agreed.

"We packed the hearing room. We'll get noticed," another protester standing near us concurred.

Yet, another protest organizer joined us outside the hearing room. So many people, so many names. At this point, I was just here for the ride.

This organizer said, "We are just so thrilled that you all are here!"

Someone else yelled, "We filled that room!"

"That will get their attention," another exclaimed.

The first organizer continued, "Exactly! We showed up today."

Several more shouts of affirmation echoed around the rotunda, their voices bouncing off the dome and reverberating around us.

The organizer smiled and started talking again, "But the day is far from over. Because the hearing room is full, I thought it would be a good idea to start organizing the next event for today. We are planning to visit every representative's office. Does everyone know who your representative is?"

Thankfully, David taught me how to check on the way to the protest. I was a constituent of Representative Mueller, a progressive White man.

For those who were unsure, the organizer quickly explained that if they typed "who is my state representative" into Google, they should be able to figure it out quickly.

Moments later, we were splitting up into groups based on state representatives. At that moment, I was the only constituent of Representative Mueller's in the whole group. Having just experienced a moment of calm and connection with something greater than me, my heart skipped a beat. The anxious and quick breathing started up again. My muscles tensed up. I reminded myself to breathe. Breathe in for four seconds, hold for four seconds, breathe out for four seconds, and hold again for four seconds, just like you taught me.

Even before I started praying for someone to join me, God answered the prayer. The organizer walked over to me and said, "I know there are several people in the hearing room who will be joining you."

She handed me a sign that just said "Representative Mueller" on it. She probably could tell I was nervous. I uttered, "Okay, sounds good!"

"I'm Gale, by the way," she said, reaching out her hand.

As we shook hands, I introduced myself too: "I'm Jason. Nice to meet you."

"Jason, I'm so happy you are here," she said with a warm smile.

"Happy to be here," I replied, my smile a bit more hesitant.

"Well, just hold this sign up when people start leaving the meeting room. And you will all walk over to the representative's office together. Thank you," she stated as she turned to walk over to the next group.

It was simple, but her smile mattered to me. It felt good to be there. And it also felt good to feel wanted.

I'd recently read a quote that went something to the effect of: "When one of the problems is isolation, merely holding a protest can address the issue." Bring people together, and they will feel less alone. It's as simple as that. The quote resonated with me deeply. I had witnessed all these people come together around a shared concern, and you could hardly feel isolated there in the Capitol yelling the same chants.

I thought about it while I waited for folks to leave the hearing room. Although the people gathered here had a mission to stop the new private prison, I wonder how many of them felt disconnected or isolated. How many people thought their efforts and voice did not matter? How many felt differently being surrounded by other protesters?

Soon enough, the proceedings ended. I later learned it was a sort of press conference, and it was all recorded. Of course, when I checked the local news the next day, it was condensed to a one-minute sound bite with about thirty seconds of the protesters' speeches and thirty seconds of a politician saying the prisons were overcrowded and the state needed more space to hold criminals. I sighed when I saw the news because it didn't, in my opinion, really inform anyone about the more complex conversations and arguments I had heard at the Capitol.

The coverage lacked any discussion about racial inequalities in the criminal justice system and how a disproportionate number of Black men were in prison for smoking some weed. And I knew plenty of White folks who frequently smoked it. The coverage also failed to mention any of the arguments about how private prisons incentivized over-sentencing so companies could make a profit. Money matters much more than fair and just sentencing. I even heard one company wanted to sue a state for not incarcerating enough people. And, of course, some of the money these companies made found its way into the coffers of politicians who pushed "tough on crime" policies, which in turn make the private prisons even more money. It was all so gross, and I doubted many folks would understand the complexities by watching their regular news program.

For instance, when we arrived at our state representative's office, a member of the staff invited us to sit in a circle in the foyer. The representative was not there, but the staff member assured us they would share our concerns with our elected official. They even had a pen and paper ready to go to jot down all of what we said.

That's when I learned Greg's horrifying story. Greg was convicted of possessing marijuana and sent to one of the other private prisons in the state. He bravely shared his story about how the prison did not and could not provide the medical care he needed. The prison had 'cut costs' to boost its profits. Greg suffered from depression and delusions. As he explained his symptoms, I was reminded of the folks I met in the psychiatric facility. All of us, whether we liked it or not, were closely supervised by trained medical professionals. Greg had no such support. He suffered alone with no one to help. As Greg spoke, the anger continued to build and fester in my stomach and chest. All I wanted to do was yell and word vomit all over the staff member. But I took a deep breath and remembered that our representative was likely to vote against the private prison. I also reminded myself not to make Greg's story about me and my feelings. Deep breaths, I told myself: in for four seconds, hold for four seconds, out for four seconds, hold for four seconds. Repeat.

Then, I wondered what effect Greg's heartbreaking story might have. If our representative was already going to vote against the bill, why were we spending this energy trying to persuade the representative to vote against the new prison?

The epiphany struck me. Greg's story was already changing me. Before I attended this day of protest, I think I had an intellectual understanding of why a new private prison would not be the greatest thing in the world. But now, my belly was filling with fire—a deep desire to stay involved in this fight. I hoped Greg's words were moving this staff member to really encourage our representative to do anything in his power to stop this prison. The story was already mattering. How could a thirty-second news segment ever cover this and do it justice?

Surprisingly enough, I learned the value of social media in spreading awareness about injustice. After we returned from the Capitol, I followed as many organizations as I could, starting with Greg's organization: F.R.E.E. Fueling Re-Entry, Empowerment, and Education.

Sadly, following all the groups meant I was one of the first to learn about what happened on Monday.

Session #28

Hey Aaron,

A lot happened in between the protest at the Capitol and the next City Council meeting in Small Rapids. You probably saw the heartbreaking news. On Monday, news broke on social media that a queer couple, two women, were denied a ride by someone driving for a ride-share app. The two said the driver "did not want queers touching his car" and that his faith prohibited him from "supporting their sinful lifestyle." The driver stranded them until they could call and get a taxi. They shared they hid that they were a couple from the driver. As you know, elsewhere, people claim their faith prevents them from making cakes for queer folks, and from making wedding dresses for queer folks, and from serving queer folks at restaurants. Theoretically, I knew this was possible, but I never anticipated how overt people would be with their hate, literally willing to lose money to discriminate. The realization stung.

The tragic discrimination fueled our fire, creating a new sense of urgency to challenge the book ban and advocate for another policy—non-discrimination ordinances protecting queer people. Not only did they not want us to be able to read about ourselves, but they also wanted to deny us services and maintain our second-class citizen status.

As soon as the news broke, I received a group text from Gloria. She suggested advocating for a non-discrimination ordinance at the City Council meeting in addition to challenging the book ban. She wanted to get as many people there as possible. I imagined the City Council meeting being flooded, so the room wouldn't hold all the people who wanted to speak. Fortunately, the City Council announced the meeting would take place during the time we would normally have had our queer discussion group at church. The news made me hopeful the whole group might be able to attend.

Pastor Esther immediately said she would make it a priority and she would attend. Jude texted that he and Naomi would attend and asked Shawn if we would like a ride. I smiled as my new community started putting things into motion. We would show up in force and advocate for justice and against discrimination. I just hoped others would attend as well.

Gloria texted to tell me she and Herald had emailed every City Council member requesting a discussion of a potential non-discrimination ordinance be added to the agenda for the meeting. Following her lead, I emailed all of them as well.

We all met for a quick bite to eat at Common Grounds, which, luckily for us, stayed open late. In addition to delicious coffee and lattes, Common Grounds had an assortment of sandwiches and soups. I was partial to the BLTA: bacon, lettuce, tomato, and avocado. As we gathered and centered ourselves for the council meeting, both Pastor Esther and Gloria said they wanted to speak. David decided he probably wouldn't receive a warm welcome, so he hoped others would speak instead of him. Naomi wanted to speak, too, and her dad had helped her write a part of her speech. She was muttering her speech to herself the whole time, revising parts and practicing them over again. Cathy and Ruth were on the fence, but it seemed like we all had a game plan and were ready to be witnesses to the events to come. Randy dressed in his suit-jacket and rainbow pin. He didn't want to speak. But he knew a little bit about the law, so he wanted to be able to correct any factually wrong claims about what the law says or doesn't say about non-discrimination.

Less than an hour later, we'd found prime, front-row seats. Luckily, we arrived a bit early because the meeting room was filling up quickly. By the time the meeting had started, the room was packed. Folks stood in the back. As I scanned the room, my heart grew as I saw a few rainbow t-shirts. A few folks wore clerical garb, which caused me a few pangs of uneasiness. I still tend to view any religious person as an anti-queer person, even as I'm sitting next to several queer-affirming Christians. And, even as I sat near a queer-affirming pastor in her clerical garb, I needed to take a moment to remind myself not all Christians condemn queer folks.

The mayor banged his gavel, something he always seemed to find some perverse satisfaction in doing, to start the meeting. He declared, "Welcome to our public comment session on the recently adopted curriculum and educational content guidance policy. We are looking forward to hearing your comments and engaging you. I do want to note that last time, some speeches did not comply with the standards for decorum and respectful engagement required in this chamber. We ask everyone to remain civil in this important discussion."

"The emails," another council member prompted.

"Oh yes, the emails. City Council members also received several emails about a proposed non-discrimination ordinance. I was hesitant to allow discussion about this topic because we do not actually have a text for the proposal. But some Council members did want to address the issue, and we will also allow for public commentary on the idea, and hopefully, we can flesh out what this idea is really all about." The mayor responded, "So, first, would any council member like to speak about the non-discrimination ordinance?"

"I do," one council member, a smartly dressed lady in her mid-forties, replied without hesitation.

"Councilwoman Baker, the floor is yours," the mayor said.

The councilwoman rose and stood at the lectern, "I'm a little wary of a proposed non-discrimination ordinance. We are a small town, and we have no money to defend such a policy in court if we need to. People might challenge it on the basis that it violates their religious freedom. Whoever wants to write the language of the proposal should work to ensure they aren't discriminating against our Christian community members."

"Maybe we need a policy protecting Christians!" Someone in the back yelled. A few people clapped in support.

It was hard not to roll my eyes. I know I'm not a legal scholar, but the argument felt so disingenuous. We can't pursue justice because people might sue? Is freedom just something you need to be rich to pay for? Something that required a well-financed legal defense?

The mayor continued as if the outburst hadn't happened. He called on another elected official.

The official, a man wearing a large cross necklace, stated, "For me, the matter of sexuality in the community is critically important. Many people want to comment on this but might be too nervous to speak publicly here. And I just do not think that we, as a council, should make this decision for the people. I hope whichever proposal is developed goes to the people for a vote. I'd like to see it as a ballot measure."

Another council member joined in, "I agree. And, frankly, I think there is a silent majority in this community who do not approve of the gay lifestyle being tossed in their face."

Before the council member could finish, someone behind me yelled, "Boo!"

I smiled, but the mayor took offense at the outburst, and he said as much. The gavel slammed down, and my ear drums took offense to the harsh clatter. The mayor exclaimed, "As I mentioned at the commencement of this meeting, we must respect the etiquette of this chamber and these proceedings. Would you like to add anything, Councilman Jefferys?"

The council member who was booed at made what I thought was an overly dramatic cough, which I found to be clearly fake.

He smiled smugly at the mayor. "Well, I think that 'boo' made my point for me. Many Christians in our community just want to live out their faith but are gosh darn afraid of being booed and attacked for just believing what they believe. I don't want a hostile movement to ruin the Christian way of life so many of our residents live."

I tasted the coppery blood in my mouth before I realized I was biting my cheek. I clenched my fists, feeling my nails piercing the skin of my palms. I've never experienced so much rage as I did in that moment. I wanted to yell! But I knew the only reaction would be the gavel assaulting my eardrums once again. Ruth reached over to me and thankfully placed her calm hand on my sewing machine leg. It was only then I realized my leg was bouncing.

I guessed I wasn't the only one angered by the completely asinine statement. Were Christians really under attack? Were they the ones experiencing rampant discrimination? Was Christian literature getting tossed out of the library? No! Were Christian students fearful of wearing their crosses to school, or was it the queer students who were anxious about the mere thought of wearing the rainbow symbol? Heck, in my experience, it was the Christian students who didn't hesitate to condemn queer folks. I remember vividly one time a self-proclaimed loving Christian yelled, "Make sure you make as much noise as you can today" on the day of silence. A day where folks were supposed to be silent to support queer students. Literally, no one was silent that day. Yet they have the audacity to pretend Christianity was under attack. In my experience, I have never felt shame or discriminated against for being Christian, other than when I worry people might associate me with the hateful, fear-mongering so-called "Christians."

However, I was continually discriminated against for being queer. I have been afraid. I have felt deep, unwavering pain.

I wanted to yell all of this at the top of my lungs, but I just sat still and mute as my blood pooled in my mouth. It tasted like I licked a copper pipe.

If I was more into conspiracy theories, I might have suspected the mayor only put the non-discrimination ordinance on the table so the council members could bash it as much as possible.

Another council member quickly stated that, "I would need to read the proposal before commenting on it. The devil is always in the details, and we can't really have a discussion until we have a proposal."

"Thank you for your thoughts; it certainly sounds to me like we need to have more specifics before we could ever consider such a policy," the mayor affirmed. "Does anyone else want to speak before we start our period of public commentary?"

We waited through the awkward pause until the mayor finally said, "Alright, now, we can open the discussion. I have a list of people who requested to speak when you all entered, and we will try to get through as much as possible. Again, I want to reiterate the need to maintain decorum; everyone should be civil in how they present their perspectives."

They called Naomi's name first.

Session #29

N AOMI FLEW OUT OF her seat and darted right for the podium. On her way up, the bright pink hair waved in the... wind? I felt a nervous energy for her, but she seemed confident enough. She had been doing what I had failed to do last time: practice. Cathy let out a quiet, "Lord, give her strength."

Apparently, God answered the prayer. I marveled at how well Naomi's speech went. Clearly, her high school public-speaking teacher knew what they were doing.

I've been wanting to speak to you all since I first heard about the proposed book ban, or the curriculum and educational content guidance policy or whatever you call it to make it sound less terrible than it is.

I went to the school district in town when I was younger. But I thank God every day that my parents let me transfer schools. I don't know if I could have survived being in high school here. I still have friends who go here, and I know they would be way too afraid to speak at a meeting like this. Sadly, they get bullied and picked on. Not all of them are queer like me, but if someone just thinks you might be gay, they ridicule you. The main thing to be concerned about is the safety of children when they are not safe. And I don't think you are doing much about it. How do you expect us to learn if we can't feel safe? If we can't be who we are?

You're all the grownups. You're the ones who are supposed to be teaching us how to talk through controversial issues and handle disagreements. Instead, you ban what you do not like. How are we supposed to learn from that? Instead of teaching us about the complexities of sexuality and the human experience, you squash it and pretend we are all the same. Instead of teaching us, you continue to force students to look elsewhere for answers and affirmations.

The question tonight is not, "Do you want queer people in this community?" There will always be queer folks here in this community. The question is not, "Do you want students to learn about queer people?" They will learn. They will find out. They will meet queer people.

No, those aren't the questions. The question is, "Do you want queer people to be able to contribute fully to this community?"

The question is, "Do you want students to learn in a safe and open environment, where they learn facts and useful information? Or do you want them to learn while surfing the web, where misinformation rules the day?"

Students will learn about sexuality and queer folk. Do you want them to learn from a stranger on the web? Or do you want them to learn from a trusted teacher—a member of the community? That's your choice.

"Mic drop," someone exclaimed as Naomi stepped away from the podium.

The gavel thundered in retaliation. The mayor exclaimed, "Again, we will make sure we respect this chamber. Please refrain from hooting and hollering. We can end this meeting at any time for additional violations."

I heard a few people muttering, maybe swearing under their breath, but the mayor called the next name.

The gentleman who rose to speak carried his Bible in hand as he approached the microphone. With a loud thud, he placed it on the podium. I saw a large, red bookmark. As he started speaking, he opened it to the bookmarked page and stated, I thought rather obviously, "I brought my Bible with me today, and I wanted to read you all a passage that should be on our minds. It comes from Genesis 19, verses 24 and 25."

"Oh, come on," Ruth muttered under her breath. Just loud enough so I could hear, but not loud enough that the City Council folks could.

The man continued slowly and deliberately, "'Then the Lord rained down burning sulfur on Sodom and Gomorrah—from the Lord out of the heavens. Thus, he overthrew those cities and the entire plain, destroying all those living in the cities—and also the vegetation in the land.' And this is what God thinks of the sin of homosexuality. He hates it. He is going to burn it out of these lands. And we will not be safe in this community if we let sin win."

"Exactly!" Someone from the back shouted. It appeared the back row was not as affirming as I could have hoped. It also seemed like they were immune from mayoral reprimands. Maybe only pro-queer outbursts lacked civility?

The mayor called Cathy next. I felt her move next to me as she lifted herself up. It took her a moment as she slowly sauntered to the podium. I'm sure some folks mistakenly assumed she was a frail, old woman, but her voice resonated with strength and love:

I did not plan on speaking tonight. I thought I had put up my marching shoes a long time ago. As you can tell, I'm an old, Black woman. I've seen my share of discrimination. When I was growing up, I couldn't go to school with the White children. We faced fire hoses and attack dogs as we worked to desegregate. Back then, City Council members, much like yourselves, often worried out loud about a Church's religious freedom to deny membership to Black folk like me. Now, I'm reading schools are banning lessons about our History. They don't want people to read books by famous Black authors. And here, you do not want people to read books by queer authors or about the Black trans folks who demanded justice.

So, I just want to say two things.

First, I hope all the kids in this community, and I can say kids because I'm just north of eighty years old, know how much God loves them. No matter what you say as elected officials, God loves queer folks and accepts them the way they are because He made them that way.

Second, I wanted to speak because I was reminded of an important thing Dr. Martin Luther King wrote so long ago it seems like a hundred lifetimes, "Injustice anywhere is a threat to justice everywhere." If you allow a rideshare driver to deny service to a gay couple, would you allow them to deny service to me? If you would allow a baker to deny service to a gay couple, would you allow them to deny service to me? And, if you would force libraries to eliminate books about queer folks, would you also ban books about people like me and the many struggles of the civil rights movement as others have tried to do? The answer, to me, seems to be yes. Thank you for your time.

"Thank you," the mayor responded hollowly.

A few more horrid speeches followed. As much as I wanted to believe these Christians, their arguments, if you could call them that, were laughable. Did they think we hadn't read Genesis 1? Had they read Galatians 3:28? *There is no longer male and female; for all of you are one in Christ Jesus.*

As the speeches continued, I noticed a little pain in my jaw where I was biting down with all my strength.

The metallic taste was still present. I remember you telling me to take deep breaths when it happens, and so I did. I'm really trying to make it a common practice for myself.

After an agonizing amount of time, when it felt like most of the speakers had come to attack same-sex relations and condemn queerness, Gloria's name was called.

I heard her take a deep breath as she stood to walk to the podium. I quickly said a little prayer for her to have the strength to say what she needed to say. Her speech went something like this:

Hello, everyone. I wanted to start off by saying that I am one of the people who emailed you about the non-discrimination ordinance. We've heard a lot tonight, but one thing that hasn't been discussed is what exactly happened. Two women were denied a service in our community because they love each other. This is what we should be focusing on. This is not some abstract idea; this is about people in our community who are being made to suffer.

But, you know, I must admit, all of this feels like a waste of my breath. Will you ever change your mind? Could you get re-elected if you did? Even if you wanted to end discrimination in our community, would you risk your political position to do so? I don't know.

I listened to a lot of you talking about how you needed to read the proposal first. This just happened. They were just discriminated against. Obviously, we could not put a proposal together. But I must ask: What do you propose? I heard a bunch of "nos" from you all, but I didn't hear what you wanted to do about this. This discrimination is happening on your watch. This is your responsibility. What do you want to do about it? What have you done about it? Many of us do not know the answer to those questions.

I've also heard a lot of people use their faith to condemn same-sex relationships. That's just heartbreaking. As a Christian woman who supports queer folks, it can be hard to believe. All it takes is a bit of research to figure out how much more complex the question of sexuality in scripture is. I encourage you all to do your research.

But, anyway, I knew I could not sit here and say nothing when discrimination was happening in our community. So, thank you for your time. I hope I didn't just waste mine.

As Gloria took her seat, the mayor called Pastor Esther's name. It was a sight to see. Pastor Esther stood, wearing her clerical garb. Her stole simply had the words "Love God, Love People" written on it. Suddenly, the Christmas song popped into my head: Now we don our gay apparel. I smiled at my strange thought, and Pastor Esther started speaking:

Thank you for allowing us to speak here tonight. It is a great honor to be here and bear witness as a servant of our

Lord. I have the great fortune of being the pastor at Central Street United Methodist Church. Our congregation is open to and loves all. I also have the great fortune of pastoring several openly queer individuals. At first, I thought it might be a challenge. I worried other members of the congregation would think less of our queer members, and I worried about whether our congregation would be divided over the issue of sexuality. We've witnessed several denominations have lively, to say the least, debates about it. Fortunately, I have found our congregation enthusiastically includes them as a member of the flock. It is simply a beautiful, divine thing.

The hardest part of my ministry has always been when people have talked to me about how hurt they have been by fellow Christians. Especially when young queer folks come and talk to me, it pains me to feel how hurt they have been by their churches, their communities, and even their parents. I've comforted queer folks who have been kicked out of their homes, and I've helped queer folks get medical attention after trying to take their own lives. It is heartbreaking every time.

I've never viewed my religious beliefs to be at odds with supporting same-sex relationships or queer people. In fact, I believe God invites all to the table, and it is our responsibility to open our arms and affirm all people, regardless of who or how they love. We are all cherished children of God. I encourage everyone in this city who claims to be Chrisitan to pray about this issue, to research this issue, and to pray some more. I have done so, and God led me to the realization that affirming queer folks, including them, and supporting them is the Christ-like thing to do. It's what I will continue to do. Thank you.

Pastor Esther stepped back from the podium, and a jeer echoed from the peanut gallery. Silence followed, and the silence spoke volumes. The mayor neither said nor did anything, yet again. The heat returned to my cheeks, and I gritted my teeth. This is nonviolent resistance, I reminded myself.

When Pastor Esther reached her seat, the mayor exclaimed, "Well, I believe we are at time, and I do not believe we had anyone else who wanted to speak. So, the meeting is adjourned."

The mayor smashed the gavel once more before turning to walk out of the room. The rest of the council followed. In a flash, my second City Council meeting was over.

I was already a little downtrodden as we left the meeting. The City Council made no firm commitments as it related to the non-discrimination ordinance, and the book ban stayed in effect. It was hard not to feel defeated. We left the building in silence and started walking back to our cars.

Then, someone decided to yell at our group, "How can you all claim to be Christians?"

I had never met this person before, and I assume he was one of the folks from the back row. Naomi's voice rang out, "Because we love Jesus Christ, and Jesus loves us."

"It is really that simple," Herald shouted back.

"Whatever, queers!" the man yelled back as he got into his car.

After he started driving away and a moment of silence, Gloria said, "And that is exactly why we need a non-discrimination ordinance."

"I hope I never have him as my taxi driver, that's for sure," I stated. I wanted my words to be sarcastic and to lighten the mood, but it didn't happen. My voice was sad; a sense of defeat oozed out.

Session #30

H EY AARON,

My mind was still racing, experiencing a full range of emotions as I arrived at Central Street the following Sunday. Whenever I tried to process the situation, my mind revved up. What I thought seemed to be the most reasonable, thoughtful, and smart arguments fell flat; nothing was changing. Our pleas failed to win any hearts or minds. We may have created even more hostility; the anti-queer folks were out in force, and their vitriol rang in my head.

Pastor Esther started the service with a warm welcome, reminding us we were all cherished children of God. Something about Pastor Esther's voice soothed me. As usual, my tear ducts stung; Ruth nudged me, a tissue in her hand. I guess when you start to release so much pain and sadness, it doesn't take much for it to want to come out.

Pastor Esther continued, "You know, one of the most heartbreaking parts of ministry is when I talk with people who have suffered because of the words and deeds of our fellow Christians."

"Amen," shouted Cathy, ironically, from the back row peanut gallery.

"Show of hands. Who here has attended Pride as a representative of our church?" Pastor Esther asked.

Several hands shot up. I looked around and saw Cathy, Ruth, Shawn, Jude, Randy, Herald, Gloria, and others, all with their hands in the air.

"What are some of your most memorable moments from attending?" Pastor Esther continued, and suddenly, it really dawned on me. Pastor Esther's sermons always had audience interactions. I had grown used to and maybe bored of all the pastoral monologues I have witnessed in my life. Pastor Esther preferred dialogues, and they sure were a lot more engaging.

"The hugs from the youth," Ruth said. "How they just need someone to say 'you are loved'."

"One time, a young man told me he thought all Christians hated him," Randy stated.

"I remember that young man. He said he was afraid of Christians," Cathy shouted from the back. "I couldn't believe how much hurt our fellow Christians caused."

"It was a tough moment," Randy replied. I noticed he was wearing his rainbow pin again.

"Heartbreaking," Pastor Esther exclaimed.

"Praying with folks, praying their families will accept them. Praying they won't get bullied," Gloria stated.

"Could we say we've witnessed a lot of hurt?" Pastor Esther asked.

"Yes," most of the congregation responded.

"But could we also say we wanted to show these folks love?" Pastor Esther continued her line of questioning.

"Yes, we can!" Ruth exclaimed as the others agreed.

"And, congregation, did you know that sometimes queer folk need support and prayer in the other eleven months of the year, not just in June?" Pastor Esther sarcastically asked.

Several folks laughed, and others exclaimed yes. I think it was at that point my tear ducts prickled again. The tears came, but they were happy tears. When did I turn into such a crybaby? Not that being one is a bad thing; perhaps I should be kinder to myself.

"I encourage us all to keep the queer people of this congregation in our prayers, and I encourage us to keep all the queer people who are suffering because of discrimination and harmful biblical interpretations in our prayers. Hear that again. They are not suffering because of harmful passages. No, they are suffering because of heteronormative *interpretations*. I encourage us to pray for the many political leaders making impactful decisions about queer rights and inclusion," Pastor Esther continued. "So, let us pray."

Pastor Esther's sermon made me even more secure being in her congregation. Whenever I enter another church, I feel like my defenses go up immediately. I ask God to protect me from Pharisees and false prophets, from harm, and from people with whips, both literal and metaphorical. I often wonder if the people around me would vote against my ability to marry or find an apartment without facing discrimination. Would they kick me out of their taxi? Would they bake me a cake? Would they come to my wedding? Would they design a website for me? Normally, I would have no idea how to answer those questions. The silence on sexuality creates anxiety.

But I can answer those questions in this congregation. I honestly do think Pastor Esther would bake a cake for me. Neither Ruth nor Cathy would kick me out of their cars. Cathy hadn't on the way to the Capital. And I'm sure David and Ruth carpool quite a bit. I bet my wedding would have a pretty good attendance from people in this congregation. No one would create a website for me because I don't think anyone in this congregation knew anything about web design. The church seriously needed someone to help them with their website.

After the service, I grabbed a cup of coffee and walked over to where Cathy and Gloria were talking.

"Jason, did you hear the good news?" Cathy asked ecstatically.

"No, I don't think so," I replied, wondering if anything had felt like good news ever since the City Council meeting.

"We did it. The new private prison isn't going to get built," Cathy exclaimed.

"Oh! Wonderful," I said. I imagined my face brightening. I also imagined it still was a little red and puffy from the bawling I had done during the service.

Cathy tempered our excitement, "It might just be because of infighting about where to put it and how to pay for it, but I still feel like we help push the issue towards justice."

"I'd like to think so. I know I learned a lot by attending and hearing Greg's story. When I met with my representative, he shared his story of being incarcerated, and it was just eye-opening," I said.

"I've heard Greg's story before, too. It is just so heartbreaking, and he is always so persuasive when sharing it," Cathy agreed.

"Do they, like, celebrate these wins?" I asked tentatively.

"Sometimes, we do. Sometimes, we have to start planning the next win. I'll keep you updated," Cathy said.

Just then, we heard Ruth's voice calling for us, "Do you all want to get lunch?"

"I could do lunch," I said instantly.

"Lunch sounds good," Gloria stated. "And we could talk about the next steps from the City Council. I'm still livid."

Cathy agreed, and we all started our walk out of the church building.

When we got to the restaurant, we were joined by quite a few folks: Pastor Esther, Shawn, Naomi, Jude, Randy, Herald, and David. The restaurant looked like it was teleported straight from the 1970s, with its checker-patterned floor and red leather booths. Gloria, Ruth, Cathy, and I ended up in the same booth while everyone else filled into the two booths behind us.

Gloria started the conversation, sounding exasperated, "I just don't understand what we are doing wrong. I feel like while we continue to have these incredibly persuasive speeches, it seems like the needle is hardly moving."

"Yeah, I felt defeated after the meeting. It almost makes me not want to go next time, honestly," I said.

"But, what else can we do? Maybe we just haven't figured out the right persuasive message," Ruth said.

"But do we think the people on the City Council are persuadable?" Ruth asked.

"What do you mean"? Gloria asked.

"It's like you said at the meeting—do you think they will ever change their minds? Or will they stick with their homophobic policies to win re-election?" Ruth said.

"I guess so. I'm not really sure. Maybe they'll never change their minds," Gloria answered.

"I doubt they ever will," I agreed solemnly.

"So, do you think going back to the City Council meetings is a waste of time?" Cathy asked Ruth.

"I didn't say that, but I think our goal shouldn't be to try to persuade the elected officials," Ruth said. "It might still be worth it to connect with other people and show folks that not everyone hates them."

"I'm not really sure what else we can do," Gloria said. "Maybe it is just hope… or false hope… but I want to believe that we change things. And this is the way we can advocate about this issue."

"Yeah, the City Council has the power, so it seems like the only way we can address the book ban and lack of a non-discrimination ordinance," I said. "But I do think you are right, Ruth. What can we do if the way we are supposed to push for change doesn't work?"

You know, theoretically, I probably knew we had other options. I'd been reading up on various social movements, and I couldn't recall ever reading about how their epic speeches to the City Council changed everything.

Ruth, however, was about to apply that theory and put it into practice. She glanced around at us all and simply said, "You know, many movements changed their strategy after the way they were supposed to advocate didn't work. Those with power want you to follow the normal process because they control the process."

Cathy continued the thought, "You want to start doing some non-violent civil disobedience?"

Ruth answered, "Maybe, but we can also start to apply economic pressure: boycotts, buy-ins, and that type of advocacy. Remember Dr. King's words, 'Tell them not to buy Wonder Bread.'"

Cathy responded, "Yes, don't buy from homophobic stores."

"Or any store that doesn't actively support queer rights," Ruth responded. "Put pressure on the business community. Make them understand hate is bad for business."

"I have read so much about the pink dollar over the past year," I said.

"The pink dollar?" Herald asked.

"Yeah, the pink dollar. I think it is just a term about how queer folks have a lot of buying power," I replied.

"Exactly! That's exactly what it is: power," Ruth said.

"Okay, I think I like this idea a lot," Gloria exclaimed.

"Yeah, take our demands to the next level," Cathy said. "Of course, we probably want to get a number of people on board, so businesses really feel the impact."

"And make it really visible which places we are boycotting," Gloria continued.

"Or we could do a buy-in. Only buy from stores which openly support queer rights." Ruth said. "Say more of a carrot approach instead of just using the stick."

My mind was racing, but in a good way. It was a feeling of nervous excitement. Somehow, I just knew we were onto something. When the normal channel for creating change didn't work, we needed to think creatively and innovate new strategies.

Later that day, I had doubts and started asking myself if the idea would work. But I caught myself and refused to let any negativity in. So, I reframed the question, in the way we've been discussing. So, instead, I asked myself: *what will it look like when it works?*

All I have to say now is... I can't wait to find out.

Session #31

"I THINK I'VE FIGURED it out!" Gloria announced at the start of our next Christian sexuality group. We really need to figure out an official name for our group.

"Figured it out?" Pastor Esther asked.

"Yes, we had been talking about how to alter our advocacy to have more influence, and I think I have an idea," Gloria answered. Sometimes, it's the small things for me. Although the stakes continued to soar, seeing Gloria excited about protesting and advocacy warmed my heart.

"Yeah, we talked about how we don't think the City Council will listen to us, no matter how well we craft our arguments," Ruth began.

"We talked about the economic power we all have and how we can use that as a part of our strategy," Cathy continued.

"Oh, I think I like where this is heading already," Randy exclaimed.

"I think it's called a buy-in, if I am not mistaken," Gloria stated, "But I am thinking about creating a group which commits to buying only from businesses displaying little rainbow flag stickers in their front window."

"I can tell you all this. She is really committed to this idea. She already ordered the stickers and has convinced one business to display one of them," Herald added.

"Oh, really? Which business?" Cathy asked.

"The Little Rapids Bistro," Gloria answered, and you could just tell she was so happy she had already convinced a business to join in.

"Is that the really fancy place downtown?" Ruth questioned.

"Yes, that's the one," Herald replied. "The owner has a queer brother and loved the idea as soon as we said it."

"Aren't they worried they will lose business?" Jude asked.

"Maybe, but they care more about this issue. And I imagine many of their clientele will be fine with this," Gloria answered. "Plus, they are a really visible business. The owner supports a lot of initiatives in town, so it will get people talking."

"So, what would we need to do to get this buy-in, if that's what we're calling it, going?" I asked.

Surprisingly, my mind felt calm. It was focused and determined. All I wanted was for this to succeed.

Pastor Esther answered first, "Well, we would probably need to have a way to show how many people are participating in the buy-in."

"Maybe we could find someone to create a website to explain our effort and list the people?" David asked.

"When we find a good web developer, we could also ask them for help with the church's website," Shawn interjected.

"I don't think I could manage creating a whole website," Naomi said. "But I do consider myself somewhat of a social media savant. I could create a group for the effort, and supporters would just need to join the group. And I could even promote the businesses who sign up to have the sticker."

"Naomi is always teaching me about social media," Jude laughed.

"I can create the group when I get home," Naomi exclaimed.

"We can work on it together, Naomi," Gloria said. "I have been writing up some drafts about how to explain the buy-in to the community."

"Sounds great!" Naomi was dancing in her chair, basically cheering and leaping for joy.

Pastor Esther said, "Thank you both for working on this. And we can all share the page for the group once it is set up."

"I'll start talking to my friends and other people I think might support us," David said.

"Me too," I echoed.

"I'll let some of the other social justice organizations in the area know what we are up to," Cathy said. "I imagine some of the folks from United in Struggle would join us."

By the time the meeting finished, the buzz of excitement was palpable. We had a plan. We all had action steps we could take to help support the queer community. We would shift the conversation and force change.

Session #32

HI AARON,

I hesitate to say it. I'm worried I'll jinx myself. But I've been feeling okay lately. I've noticed myself smiling a bit more. I'm continuing to surround myself with community. I'm developing new friendships. I just feel like I've got a lot of forward momentum, you know? I was thinking about it the other day, and it has been a while since a mass shooting. Things seem to be getting better. We've even made a lot of progress on our buy-in campaign.

By the time Sunday rolled around, Gloria and Naomi had already finalized and shared their initial draft for the buy-in. Scratch that, they created an entire written framework for the effort, including a statement of our mission and a pamphlet to pass out to persuade people to join. They also came up with a name: Love Triumphs.

I adore that name. It already implies we can win and we're on the right side of this fight. We were on the side of love and calls for love would continue to sound in Small Rapids. The mission statement reads,

The Small Rapids City Council continues to assault what should be the shared values of diversity, inclusion, justice, and love. The efforts to ban books and stop non-discrimination policies violate the basic principles of liberty and the Golden Rule: Do unto others as you would have them do unto you. Would our community accept banning heterosexual books? Would our community allow straight couples to be denied services? We think not. The ongoing discrimination in our community requires an innovative response. If the City Council will not listen to our pleas, we must advance our cause in a way that people will witness and feel. Thus, we have launched a new initiative called Love Triumphs. We call on all people in Small Rapids and beyond to patronize only those businesses who will sign our equality pledge and commit to displaying a small rainbow sticker in their windows. The people of Small Rapids, as evidenced by all of those who have testified to the City Council, want to be on the right side of history. We want to support and affirm our queer friends, family members, and neighbors. Our growing movement will not stop until Love Triumphs in Small Rapids and beyond.

Not too bad for a first draft. After church, we stayed in the sanctuary to plan our next steps. We formed a circle big enough for everyone, and David plopped down next to me. A few other folks stayed behind to hear about what we were doing. By this time, I had been slowly learning a bit about the other folks in the congregation. One of the women who stayed was an elderly, rather short, white woman. She had lost her husband of over thirty years earlier in the year. A part of me thought she just wanted company. That all changed when she first spoke, "I'm sorry I haven't joined you all yet. I've just been having a rough time. But I want to help if I can."

Her voice lingered for a moment, downtrodden and almost defeated. Ruth responded, "Well, we are more than happy to have you now, Tina."

"You have to take care of yourself first," Cathy echoed.

"You can't pour from an empty cup, you know?" David nodded toward Cathy.

"I know," Tina replied with a rather large sigh. "But I shouldn't be the center of attention. I just want to get involved and get caught up to speed on this dreadful Small Rapids business. So sad."

As Tina was speaking, David leaned closer to me and whispered, "One of her nieces is queer."

"You've come to the right place," Naomi exclaimed. "I'm so excited to share what we have been thinking about."

"Let's get started, shall we?" Pastor Esther said as she re-entered the sanctuary.

Naomi jumped right into explaining all she'd done to build out a social media presence for Love Triumphs.

She had created a page with a beautiful rainbow banner with Love Triumphs in bold, dark lettering. For now, the page was private and hidden. That way, we could invite only people we knew and only those who committed to our mission. Naomi explained it like this: the page would be our virtual staging area before our campaign went public. We wanted to gather support before the trolls started their digital bombardment.

Gloria had also created cute commitment cards with small rainbow stickers in the bottom right corner. People just needed to fill out their names to get added to the list of people who were participating in the buy-in and agree to their name being displayed publicly. She also created separate commitment cards for the businesses pledging to support our mission, and they got their sticker when they signed their commitment card. Gloria created an email address for Love Triumphs, and every single piece of material we produced would have the email address on it. Gloria said, hopefully, it would not be too difficult to make businesses aware of the buy-in and find a few that wanted to join in the action.

"We thought we could go public after we have 200 supporters," Naomi said. "That should be enough people to show our economic power, right?"

"I would think so," I responded hesitantly.

"Sure! Everything looks so great," David said. "You all did a wonderful job."

"I agree," Randy said. "Thank you for working on it."

"Well, none of it is perfect. We just wanted to get some thoughts down," Gloria stated.

"I think it is simply wonderful," Shawn said, wearing his usual Target shirt. "Thank you both."

"So, can we start inviting people to join our social media page?" Pastor Esther asked.

"Yup, you should be able to," Naomi responded.

"Awesome! I'll try to join in a couple of minutes, and I'll start inviting folks," Pastor Esther stated.

"I might just consider getting a social media account," Ruth laughed. "I'm just so proud I avoided it for so long."

"I'll start inviting people from United in Struggle," Cathy said. "I know a few of them will be interested in this."

"Do we need anyone to start contacting businesses?" I asked.

"I've asked a few already," Gloria replied. "But we can certainly contact more."

"Let's try to create a little list before we leave," I said.

"Sounds good," Gloria exclaimed.

"I already made a list of people who I can contact," David said.

Our meeting ended rather quickly. We had all our action steps, and the excitement was too much to contain. We all wanted to get to work. Later that day, I found myself in Common Ground with my list from Gloria, typing up an email I could send to the business owners:

Greetings, I am messaging you as a representative of the newly formed group, Love Triumphs. Recent public deliberations involving sexuality have forced the hands of queer folks and their allies in our communities. We simply cannot continue to support those who do not support everyone in the community. We cannot continue as usual when discrimination occurs in town. As such, we are launching a buy-in campaign. The members of our group will only patronize businesses that openly support queer rights. We will not financially support people who do not support our right to exist in Small Rapids. We hope you will join us by becoming one of the businesses showing open support of queer rights by displaying a small rainbow sticker by your front door. If you are interested in showing your support, please respond to this message to let us know. I appreciate your consideration!

I'm not going to lie. I really struggled to write the email, and I wasn't sure what I wanted to say. I felt like the message was okay, but I had already anticipated the backlash. Just thinking about what people might say made typing that much more difficult. But I did it; I pushed through it. I just kept reminding myself I wanted to be the person I used to need; someone willing to risk their reputation and take a stand for equality, love, and queer rights.

Moments later, I heard a familiar voice, and my head snapped up so I could look to see who it was. David had entered, still in his Sunday best. For the first time, my eyes wandered down to check out his behind. Well, they didn't have to wander that far. David had fairly tight black dress pants on, and his belt really helped accentuate the area. He stood there waiting in line, and I couldn't tell if he had noticed me.

I awkwardly kept looking up to see how quickly the line was moving. And it moved rapidly. That's what happens when only three people place orders. As soon as David started looking around for a spot, I waved at him. It took him a moment, but he saw me. He nodded at me and had one of those "well, duh" expressions on his face. He smiled and started walking over to me.

"Hey, Jason. Long time no see," he laughed.

"I know, right?" I responded with a smirk of my own.

"Can I join you?" he asked.

"Of course. Have a seat," I answered. "I'm working on stuff for the buy-in."

"I want to work on that, too," he said as he grabbed a chair.

Suddenly, I felt like I was smelling a campfire. I asked, "That smells good. What did you get?"

"Oh, a toasted marshmallow latte. It's my go-to when I want a little pick-me-up," David replied.

"It has been a while since I've smelled one of those," I stated.

David must have registered the hint of bittersweetness in my voice, and not just his latte, because he inquired, "Why is that?"

"I... it's nothing. Don't worry about it." I answered.

"You sure?" David asked. He must have noticed how unconvinced I was.

"It is just that," I sighed deeply. "It was Mario's favorite drink."

"Mario had really good taste then," David continued without missing a beat. "Do you miss him?"

I hesitated for long enough, so David filled the void, "We don't have to talk about this if you don't want to."

"No, we can," I started. "It's just hard."

"I know," David sighed. "Do you remember Karla Clausen?"

"Yeah, vaguely," I said honestly. "She was on the team with you, right?"

"Yeah, she was. I learned so much from her. She was so smart, and I just know she could have qualified for nationals." David's voice was slow and solemn. "I do miss her. Every time I hear about a debate tournament.

Every time I use one of the research tips she taught me. I think about her every day."

I let out another deep breath before I spoke, "I miss Mario so much. I miss his smile. I miss how he just cared for everyone. I miss how he loved people and just wanted them to be happy. I miss holding his hand and hugging him. I miss talking with him about our faith and how beautiful queer love could be. I miss his love and warmth. And I am just so pissed we never had the chance to share it all with people. I just want to yell at God for taking him from me. I get so angry that I can barely breathe."

"And you think of Job and wonder why God is testing you. Why is God making bets with the devil while you suffer? And you wake up day after day hoping everything will be different, but it's not." David interjected. Was he reading my mind?

"Yeah, exactly," I stated, stunned that David could finish my thought so easily.

"I still have days where I hope this is all just a horrible nightmare, and I'll wake up in some utopia where life is just so much easier," he stated.

"And it hurts every time you remember the horrible nightmare is your reality," I continued.

"Exactly," he replied.

We fell silent for a moment, both succumbing to the weight of our combined trauma. My mind saw everything—maybe for the first time—the interconnected webs of how the shooting continued to impact people. Whether they were there, knew someone who was there, or knew someone who knew someone who was there, thousands of people were affected by that day. I imagined all the links connecting those people, and I saw how we became traumatized and how we are all still processing and healing from it. The words just slipped out of my mouth, "How do we keep moving forward?"

"Our small hope is one day, things will be better, and we can be that change," David replied.

"For all the future Marios and Karlas?" I asked.

"For all the future Marios and Karlas," he answered. "For me, finding Central Street helped a lot. We've found a community of people who want to make things better, too. I've talked a lot with Ruth, Cathy, Pastor Esther, Shawn, and Gloria these past few years about finding hope in times of despair, finding purpose in pain, and finding love in a world full of hate. I'm so thankful you found your way to us."

"I am, too," I replied. "I haven't felt this good in a while. And I'm thankful for them, you, and what we are doing."

"So, let's finish up our messages," David said. "What do you say?"

"Sounds great to me," I said. "One question: Can you read over what I wrote?"

"Of course! Let me see," David exclaimed, and I handed over my laptop. My stomach tightened; I imagined it had turned into a pretzel as I waited for David to finish. My blood pressure always skyrockets when people scrutinize my work. But, within a couple of minutes, David said he loved it and couldn't wait for people to read it. With David's seal of approval, close to a dozen local businesses would soon find the message in their inboxes.

I stayed to help David with his messages, too. By the next day, the Love Triumphs group page already had over 100 members. One hundred and fifty folks had signed up to participate in the buy-in by Tuesday. Love Triumphs seemed to be growing at an exponential rate.

Session #33

H I AARON,

Remember last week when I was telling you about how it felt strange to go without a mass shooting for so long? Sadly, I guess it was some type of premonition. As I am sure you saw on the news, another one happened. Our interconnected web of folks traumatized by school shootings grew again. Another nineteen people were killed. Others have severe injuries. Canyon View High School's community will never be the same.

Within minutes of hearing about it, I felt the rage bubbling from the pit of my stomach. I started feeling like I needed to throw up. My skin began itching, like an army of ants started crawling all over me. Then, I reminded myself to do my breathing exercises. I took the deep breaths you taught, and I counted five things that I could see. Just like we had talked about, I thought of four things I could hear. That was trickier because

I only noticed the humming of my refrigerator. But I worked through the steps—it helped.

I've been working on caring for myself since I found out about the shooting. I have given myself permission to feel all I want to feel. I have let myself do what I feel like doing. If I want to yell, I let myself yell. If I want to cry, I cry. If I want a milkshake, I just get one and inhale its delicious, normally caramel, goodness. I just let myself do what I feel like I need to do. No judgment.

Some folks have already started organizing marches and protests. Of course, I want to go. I think I need a sense of community. Nothing's happened since the last shooting, and I doubt anything will happen before the next. But I want to join others who are at least calling for change. The public lament heals. It's the idea of community being the solution to isolation we talked about. I feel like I want to isolate myself from the world, but I also know that seeing others and seeing the people from Central Street helps.

I knew it would help because it was like a warm hug when people contacted me. I hadn't heard from my mom in a while. She was the first one to text me, wanting to check in and see how I was doing. Pastor Esther and Ruth texted me, too, telling me they were praying for me. David's text was a long rant about how much this sucked and how awful it was that we were going to go through this again.

I also feel like I've been on repeat. I've been saying the same things that I said after the last shooting. People said things would be different this time, just like last time. People have called for common-sense gun legislation, just like last time. More people are buying guns because they are worried about restrictive legislation, just like last time. People are talking about having more security at schools, just like last time. People are talking about how only the United States has such a severe gun violence problem, just like last time. And, of course, people are scapegoating Chicago, just like last time, even though this shooting occurred in Texas.

Like every time, folks pointed out, we are simply working our way through the same, tired script. In doing so, they faithfully read the lines of their unaltered script for our unending production.

However, for me, things were different this time. I had a community of people as a good number of people from Central Street United Methodist Church wanted to attend. On the day of the protest and march, we all met at church to carpool to the protest site.

Pastor Esther wore her clerical garb and her "Love God, Love People" stole. Herald and Jude both created signs saying, "Gun Owners for Gun Control." I was a bit stunned. I had to reread their signs because I had no idea either of them owned guns. I thought back to the previous march and the speaker who talked about being a gun owner. I couldn't recall if Herald or Jude were there, too.

In part, I felt a tad concerned about the signs. I know they were powerful because their gun ownership gave them a different sort of credibility. They knew guns. They owned guns. They were not afraid of gun control. And I believe that mattered, and their voices mattered.

But why do you have to own a gun to get this type of credibility? Do those of us who have survived gun violence get the same sort of credibility? Suddenly, I wished I had created a sign which said, "Gun Violence Survivor for Gun Control." Maybe something like "I Survived a School Shooting. Ask Me About It." I knew the last one was too long, but I wondered what people would think. I decided to try and make a sign that night, so I would have it for the next march, because we all know there will be another shooting.

Naomi's sign read, "I don't want to die in school." Simple. Poignant. Powerful.

Randy's sign read, "Look up Isaiah 1:15-17!"

Honestly, I had to ask him what the passage was all about, only to discover he had created little printouts of the verse he could pass out. After handing one to me, he said, "I'm sick and tired of hearing those with power pretend to do something about it and pretend they are praying."

I looked down at the passage, and it read, "When you spread out your hands in prayer, I hide my eyes from you; even when you offer many prayers, I am not listening. Your hands are full of blood! Wash and make yourselves clean. Take your evil deeds out of my sight; stop doing wrong."

Somehow, Randy must have known how quickly I could read. The second I finished reading, he stated, "So many political leaders have blood on their hands. They lift their hands to pray, and I all see blood-soaked hands."

"Yeah, that's...," I paused for a second while taking in the image. I imagined Senators stopping debates and discussions on how to address gun violence. I remembered how representatives opposed even studying gun violence as a public health issue. I saw the blood on their hands, too. "Powerful."

"Don't get me wrong, Jason. I believe in prayer," Randy continued, "But I also believe that, in this case, God has answered our prayers. We just have to be willing to accept His answer and do something. God wants us to do something."

"Makes sense to me," I replied. "I hope someday we'll actually be willing to do something."

"Me too," Randy stated. "I pray we find the courage."

A few moments later, we got into the vehicles. When we arrived, we were thirty minutes early, but the park in front of City Hall was already packed. We gathered across the street. We would still have a perfect view of the platform constructed the night before, although it would make sense just to leave it as a permanent fixture of the park. It's had a lot of use lately.

As we waited for the speeches to start, Gloria gathered us together just to confirm we would wait another week or two before launching the Love Triumphs campaign. We felt we had enough people to launch, but we didn't want to compete with or undermine the ongoing gun violence advocacy. I agreed. It is hard enough to get people to notice you and your message.

We chit-chatted until a speaker, a rather large Black man who wore a dark grey suit with a blue button-up shirt and tie, approached the podium. I thought I knew him, or at least had seen him before.

Cathy must have either felt my confusion or seen it on my face because she whispered to me, "That's Reverend Randall. He is a part of United in Struggle."

Recognition suddenly dawned on me. I asked, "He was at the prison advocacy day at the Capitol?"

"Yup, sadly, we never got a chance to introduce you to him," Cathy replied. "We'll fix it sometime."

"Okay, sounds good!" I said just as Reverend Randall started.

"Welcome, everyone. I am happy to see so many of you here, but deeply saddened these meetings continue to be necessary," Reverend Randall's deep bass voice boomed throughout the crowd. Not hard to tell he was a preacher.

"We gather here today to protest gun violence in a place of gun violence," Reverend Randall stated, squaring his shoulders and gripping the lectern.

"A place of gun violence?" The question just slipped out.

"Yes. Trey," Cathy whispered.

"As many of you know, nearly ten years ago, Trey Sanders was killed by a police officer in this very park," the Reverend said solemnly.

"That's right," Ruth uttered.

"Well, we have work to do, don't we?" Reverend Randall asked. A few people shouted yes, but apparently, their shouts were not enough to satisfy the reverend.

"Now, I'm a big believer in audience participation, so let's try that again," he stated, "We have some work to do, don't we?"

"Yes!" More of the crowd cheered, but I knew this many people could be much louder.

Reverend Randall continued, "Okay, we'll keep working on that. For now, raise your hand if you know someone who was lost to gun violence."

David's hand shot up instantly, and my hand reacted a bit slower. For a second, I thought our hands would be the only ones in the air. Slowly but surely, other hands snuck tentatively into the sky. So many broken souls raised their hands, showing they, too, had suffered from gun violence. I looked around, noticing Ruth with her hand up, too. Within a minute, I guess just over half of the protesters gathered had raised their hands.

It was a heartbreaking display, and we showed the damage and harm gun violence has left in its wake. We were the points in the interconnected web of the traumatized. All the lost lives, all the hurt and all the grief, was visualized in a single snapshot of the population of Big Rapids. I imagined other protests throughout the nation, all those people with raised hands. All affected by gun violence in some way—our identities molded by horror.

I'm sure you can already guess that I was crying. Crying is becoming pretty much my Modus Operandi. I looked over to David; tears worked their way down his face, too. Ruth and Pastor Esther displayed their damp cheeks for all to see.

"I imagined many of you would raise your hands," Reverend Randall continued. "Did you know more children and teens die from gun violence than car crashes and cancer?"

"Yes!" The crowd yelled—their voices raw with ferocity.

"Don't you find it incredibly disturbing?" he shouted at them.

"Yes!" The crowd screeched.

"Some people believe owning a killing machine is their God-given right, but did you know Jesus was not, in fact, a member of the NRA?" Reverend Randall exclaimed.

I snorted a bit.

"Did you also know many of the people who tweet about their thoughts and prayers actually have the power to do something?" Reverend Randall continued. "They could be the answer to all our prayers today. They *could* pass common-sense gun safety regulations. They could have done that the last time we witnessed the horrors of yet another mass shooting."

"That's right!" Ruth exclaimed as the crowd cheered.

"Now, I know not everyone here is Christian like I am. We all gather here for many different reasons, but our mission is the same. No matter what you believe, you know every life is sacred, and it is our duty as a community to address the carnage we continue to witness. Today, we demand political leaders do something to safeguard our communities. I do not want to continue watching yet another group of kids cut down before they have barely started living their lives,"

Reverend Randall exclaimed, earning another round of applause.

"So, we are going to march. For me, marching is my prayer. It is my prayer for safer communities, it is my prayer that political leaders do something, and it is my prayer for an end to all gun violence. It is my prayer that no one else needs to die to show our political leaders they must act. They must pass gun safety legislation. And they needed to do it yesterday! Let us march!"

The crowd roared in approval. In the blink of an eye, we saw the start of the procession filing away from city hall. I blurted out, "That was quick. I thought there would be more speeches."

"Maybe there will be some at the end?" David said.

The chants had already started. "Hey, hey, ho, ho, gun violence has gotta go!"

Randy, Pastor Esther, David, and everyone else started to cross the street. I was about to follow them, but I heard Ruth's hesitant voice.

"Hey, I don't think I'm going to be able to walk it all."

"We really need to start remembering to bring you a wheelchair," Cathy exclaimed.

"It's alright. You all just go on ahead. I'll wait here," Ruth replied.

"I can stay here with you, Ruth," I said.

"No, you go on ahead, Jason," Ruth said. "I know how much this issue means to you."

"It means a lot to you too, Ruth," Cathy said. "We don't want to leave you alone."

"Exactly, being in a community is what matters most right now," I stated, perhaps a little more firmly than I intended.

I noticed David and Pastor Esther looking back at us from across the street. I raised my pointer finger and mouthed, "One second."

"We could drive to the end of the route together," Cathy suggested.

"We can try," Ruth said. "I bet traffic will be a nightmare."

"We'll face it all together," I responded.

Cathy must have caught sight of David and Pastor Esther because she yelled, "We are going to drive."

In union, David and Pastor Esther mouthed okay and turned to join the procession. As they did, the chant changed: "Hey there, NRA, how many kids have you killed today!"

The rest of the group had already started marching down the route. We watched them go for a moment, and then Ruth, Cathy, and I returned to the cars.

I will never forget the conversation I had with Ruth and Cathy.

Session #34

"CAN I ASK YOU why gun violence means so much to you, Ruth?" I asked as we climbed into the car.

"Sounds like you just did," Ruth laughed before becoming much more serious. "But you shared with me all about Mario, so I can share with you about Donnie."

"Oh, Donnie," Cathy exclaimed, the pain clear in her voice.

"Donnie was my grandson," Ruth began. "He was such a good boy, always staying out of trouble. He was so smart, and he was going to go to college. I was so proud of him. But, one night, gun violence took his life, too. Like so many people, he became a gun violence statistic. Don't get me wrong. He will always be more than a statistic to me. But, whenever you read a number about how many people have died due to gun violence, he is a part of that number."

"I... I'm so sorry to hear that," I replied. For a moment, I just wanted to feel numb. I read somewhere sometimes, when we experience so much trauma, we just don't want to feel anymore. But I wanted to feel for Ruth. I knew she felt for me when I told her about Mario.

"Me too, Jason. Me too," Ruth continued. "The police said he died because of a shootout. A bunch of police were trying to bust a drug deal or something. Things went downhill fast. The drug dealers opened fire, and the police returned it. Donnie was not a part of any of it, but some of the bullets must have strayed and hit my son and daughter-in-law's house. They shattered the window to his room, and he was hit. A stray bullet killed him before the shooting stopped."

"It is just awful," Cathy expressed. "Not even safe in your own home."

"He was doing everything he needed to do, but it wasn't enough. In his own home," Ruth said. "It's still difficult to process even eight years later."

I had no idea what to say. I thought about what I'd wanted people to say to me about Mario after his death. Slowly, I whispered, "I'm so sorry for your loss, Ruth. When Mario died, I thought it would always hurt. But, sometimes, like today, I feel him with me, and I find comfort in that."

"Oh yes, Donnie is with me. I have been feeling his presence all day. He's a little warmth amid all the dark and cold. It's taken a while, but now I remember him fondly every day. It's always bittersweet, but more often than not, his memory puts a smile on my face. Did you know the memories of those we lose are etched into the synapses of our brains?" Ruth said. "We literally cannot go anywhere without them."

"Amen," Cathy said.

"And just being here honors them. I do believe each and every time we do something to make a better world; we honor all of those we've lost," Ruth steadfastly proclaimed.

"I believe that too," I responded. I closed my eyes and took a deep breath. It felt like I was breathing in his warmth, his glow, his brightness. "Remembering Mario hurts. But I know I wouldn't be able to feel his joy, his happiness, and his love without thinking of him and feeling the hurt."

"Exactly, we can't remember the good without the bad. As time goes on, the bad stings less and less. And we remember more and more of the good. There's always some pain there, but I wouldn't give up my memories of Donnie for anything," Ruth continued. "Like the time I went to his spelling bee at school. The school made a big production out of it. We were in the auditorium and everything. He did so well—won second place, in fact. He messed up the word 'phlegm,' saying 'f' instead of 'ph.' I was annoyed they picked that particular word. But he always remembered how to spell it correctly afterward. I'll never forget how proud I was."

"We all have our little stories, don't we?" Cathy stated. "Moments where we just feel something so deeply about someone else, our friends, family, kids, romantic partners. You name it. We all have these magical moments we want to last forever, and we want to remember forever."

"Yes, I guess we do," I said, thinking of the Valentine's date I planned.

"It is those moments that keep me going," Ruth said. "When you get to my age, going to funerals basically becomes your main social activity. But I hang onto the good times, and I know I can help make the world a better place so others can have more and more of them."

"And less and less of the bad times," Cathy replied. "Like dealing with racism or sexism or homophobia or gun violence."

"I like how you said that a moment ago, Ruth—we honor them when we advocate for change, for a better world," I replied. "One with less pain and suffering."

"Well then, let's go honor them," Ruth exclaimed as we arrived at the end of the route. In the distance, we could see the procession coming towards us. We got out of the car, already hearing the chants moving closer and closer.

"Hey, hey, ho, ho, gun violence has gotta go!"

I smiled, thankful for every single person marching for a better world.

Session #35

Aaron! Guess what!?

Love Triumphs launched its buy-in campaign this week. It all happened much more quickly than we anticipated, which just goes to show how connected everyone was. We had nearly 400 signatures from people who agreed to only shop at stores displaying a rainbow sticker. That's over 200 more committed queer folks and their allies than the initial goal. The newspaper included our call to action as a letter to the editor. With our social media page now public and visible for anyone to see, we started getting more and more likes and follows on our post announcing the buy-in. Over 100 people shared the buy-in information on social media, creating a fair number of nasty posts..

Gloria, Naomi, and Cathy all engaged with them, refuting their every attack point by point. Greg—the man from the prison protest—even posted a few words of affirmation. Many more people from both Small

Rapids and beyond joined in, passionately arguing for inclusion and equity.

Sadly, at first, I only knew of two businesses that had their rainbow stickers ready to go. The first was Common Grounds. The second was the fancy Bistro right in the center of town; Gloria and Herald were close friends with the owner. Personal pressure matters, I guess.

But, the next day, my heart broke. The Golden Skillet released a statement on social media condemning the Love Triumphs campaign. The post said the following, "At the Golden Skillet, we pride ourselves on preparing delicious and cost-friendly meals for our friends and families in the community. Unfortunately, outside agitators have started to attack our core family values and are working to financially ruin any business living out its Christian beliefs. We want to be clear—we will not succumb to the pressure to fit within the ungodly culture peddling its "beliefs" in our town. Fellow Christians, we will always have our doors open for you and your family."

I drove past the restaurant later in the day and noticed the massive signs. Instead of putting a little rainbow on their door to show they wanted everyone's money, they placed two signs on both sides of the entryway. One said, "Pro-Christian," and the other said, "Pro-Family." It's always seemed strange to me that people interpret any queer-affirming message as anti-Christian and anti-family. All I wanted was to live my life as a proud and open queer Christian who wanted a family someday. But sadly, whenever I hear these antiqueer messages about gays being inherently unchristian, I wonder if I should even consider myself a Christian. I believe in Christ, but I cannot and do not believe in the church and other Christians, especially when they continue to attack me and those like me. How can I associate myself with these people who are so un-Christlike?

The Golden Skillet's actions felt like a knife to the heart. It was so hard not to think about all the times I sat in a booth there with Mario, and we just laughed. Or we talked about something serious. Or he got some frosting on his chin, and he sensually tried to lick it off, which inevitably meant we started chuckling like the teenage boys we were.

I will always admit their cinnamon rolls taste delicious. They are just amazing. I admit that I am craving those cinnamon rolls as I write to you; I really desire the gooey goodness. But then, I remember the owners hold explicitly anti-queer views and explicitly wanted me to have fewer rights. I mean, I am sure they would still take my money if I kept my queerness in check and invisible. As I think about the restaurant now, I still feel the sting of their decision to exclude me. What hurts even more is all the people who decided that a tasty cinnamon roll mattered to them more than my rights, my safety, and my happiness.

I also must admit, if I had been Golden Skillet's financial consultant, I might have recommended they emphasize their conservative, family values. In our town, it was hardly a risk. Siding with the majority and attacking the minority worked well to build one's brand. I mean, if I was a person with no morals and if I did not care for all of God's creation, I would have found what they did to be a savvy and smart business move. In the days that followed, the restaurant was packed. It was normally really busy, but I wondered how anyone found parking whenever I drove past. It was beyond busy. They must have been making bank. They commodified their faith; they reduced their faith into a savvy, business move. And it worked.

You may say I was enacting some type of self-punishment ritual driving past, and you might be right. I drove past a few times on purpose just to find out what was going on. Every time, I regretted my decision, as I was either filled with anger or sadness about how much more business they seemed to be getting. I was worth less than a cinnamon roll.

Common Grounds was way more in my price range than the Bistro. I tried to stop there as much as I could to support them. That usually brought a smile to my face. Even with the rainbow sticker, they seemed busy—extremely busy. With only two rainbow stickers around town, those three hundred or so people must have been boosting the Common Grounds profits. Of course, when I think about it, I wonder if having the sticker was a financial decision on their part. Did they think they would corner the market on the rainbow dollar? Because they certainly have done. Heck, I might just be happy someone recognizes we are here, we are queer, and we have money. Well, I don't have that much, but Gloria and Herald are well off.

In fact, right after the buy-in started, I went to Common Grounds. It was packed. Normally, it was busy. But, on that day, I couldn't find a spot to sit. Frankly, it annoyed me. Usually, I could just walk in, order, and find a nice spot to sit. Not that day. The line was all the way out the door.

The BLTA (Bacon, Lettuce, Tomato, Avocado) had been changed to the LGBT (Lettuce, Guacamole, Bacon, Tomato). As much as I knew it was a superficial gesture, I had to have one. Both Common Grounds and the Golden Skillet had invited us to purchase and consume based on our identities and beliefs. Many people did. Although lots of people decided to stuff their faces with hate for me and the rest of us queers.

But this line was full of people who wanted to grab a bit to eat and affirm queer people like me.

A semi-brilliant idea popped into my head. I took a quick picture of all the people waiting to send to some of the businesses that we had never heard back from. Maybe to advance queer rights, I would have to play the financial game? Wave a few rainbow dollars in their faces? The whole strategy made me feel a bit icky, but what felt worse was imagining it might work.

Fortunately, I did not need to wait long to find out.

Session #36

H EY AARON,

I had a wonderful week. Well, at least I have a bright spot I can barely wait to share with you. Honestly, I feel proud of myself. I don't want to get a big head or anything, but I got another business to join in with the Love Triumphs campaign.

It all started with an email from a business named Frank's Automotive Repair, replying to my message with the picture of the incredibly long line at Common Grounds. The owner, Frank, said he wanted to meet up and talk about joining the movement. He did have a few concerns he wanted to discuss first. I texted David to see if he wanted to go with me. Thankfully, he did.

The next day, David picked me up just before noon. Before I had my seatbelt on, he asked, "You ready for this?"

"Yeah, actually, I think I am," I replied.

"Well, you certainly dressed to impress," David said with a sly grin.

"Of course, I want to look like a respectable homosexual today," I answered with a little chuckle.

"Dapper, I think they call that dapper," David said.

"You look dapper, too," I said. "You're even wearing a tie."

"Like you said, dress to impress," David replied.

"So, you said!" I exclaimed.

"Oh yeah," he replied. "But seriously, don't we look handsome?"

I couldn't disagree, "Yeah, we do."

A moment later, a large red and blue sign with "Frank's Auto" in big, black bold letters greeted us. The repair shop was on the outskirts of town, on a street which leads out into the country. I couldn't recall passing it before. The building was much smaller than I thought it would be. I don't know much about how automotive repair works, but it only looked like it had room for two cars in the garage.

As soon as we parked, a man with the typical automotive repair outfit and accompanying oil stains basically jolted out of the front door.

"Welcome, I'm Frank!" he exclaimed as soon as we stepped out of David's car.

"Hi!" David and I responded in unison.

"Come on in," Frank said. "I would shake your hands, but mine are pretty dirty right now."

"Maybe some other time," David laughed.

"Deal," Frank said as he opened the door for us.

A second later, we were sitting in his disorganized office. He had stacks of paper and cans of Diet Coke everywhere. Recognizing this, he uttered, "Sorry for the mess, you guys. It is hard to keep up with just me and one other employee."

"It is all good," David responded. "My schoolwork is in a constant state of disarray."

"School work?" Frank asked.

"Yup, we're both working our way through college at Big Rapids University," I replied. "Hard to believe we are almost done with our second year already."

"Well, good for you. My son is only a sophomore in high school. But he has already decided to move all the way to Chicago for college," Frank continued, and it was not hard to miss the sad note in his voice.

"And you don't want him to move so far away?" David asked.

"It will be hard. I feel like I'm bracing for it already. It has just been the two of us for a while now. His mother died when he was pretty young. It was rough, but we figured out how to make it work," Frank stated. "But, anyway, that's not entirely why you're here, but a part of it."

"Yeah?" David questioned.

"Yep, I think this is still on a need-to-know basis. I don't think he wants anyone to know, and I probably shouldn't be telling you, but my son is gay. He came out to me last year. I know he's struggled a lot in this community already. All this discourse around the book bans and discrimination hasn't helped. I know that one of the reasons he wants to move all the way to Chicago is to find a more tolerant...err..., I mean, affirming community," Frank responded soberly. "I'm still getting used to the language and all of that, but it breaks my heart he doesn't want to live in this town anymore. But I honestly can't blame him."

"It is hard to live here sometimes," I affirmed. "Please let me know if he ever needs anything."

"We are sort of experts in being gay in this city," David nodded with another little laugh.

"I will, but he also has Zach. That's the other mechanic working here. He's on his lunch break," Frank stated. "He is gay, too, and he is okay with people knowing. I think Zach is the reason my son, Tim, was willing to come out to me. I can't imagine Tim would have unless he knew I was trying to be a supportive ally and boss or whatever."

"I'm sure it helped," I said. "I'm glad he has you."

"Yeah, when I saw the post about starting the buy-in, I thought about them for quite a while," Frank said. "I really wanted to do it for them."

"Sounds like a great reason to me," David exclaimed.

"Two great reasons, actually," Frank interjected. "I care for them both so much. They are all I have."

"If you don't mind me asking, what is the holdup then?" I asked rather abruptly. I immediately worried I was being too aggressive, so I reminded myself to take a deep breath. I refused to let myself feel too anxious or angry; I wanted this to work. We needed Frank's support.

"Well, this business is all that's keeping us afloat. We get by, but barely. I have no idea how we are going to afford college, especially if he moves. I really can't afford to lose customers. We can't afford to be polarizing," Frank replied somberly. My body felt his pain, angst, and indecisiveness with every word. Like all of us, he knew the risks of being open and affirming in this town. I was lost for words. How could we ask someone to put themselves in peril of losing everything? Fortunately, David knew exactly what to say.

"I don't know about that, Frank. Being more polarized seems to be working for Common Grounds, and it is working for Golden Skillet. They both have just been packed since this buy-in started," David stated firmly.

"And the Bistro downtown is doing just fine," I added, David's words inspiring me. His confidence oozed out with every word. "Remember the picture I sent you. Common Grounds is as busy as it has ever been."

"Yeah, maybe you're right," Frank stated. "But I'm scared. This is what I have. It keeps me afloat, and it helps with my son's college bills, and we've already been struggling."

"Frank, can I be honest with you?" I said suddenly.

He seemed a bit startled by my abruptness but still answered, "Of course."

"I honestly don't think I'd heard of your business until we started this campaign. For me, the four automotive repair places in the area all bleed together. I don't have any rhyme or reason for why I go to the one that I go to. But now, I do. I know I am supporting someone who wants to support me. I know I'm supporting two other queer folks, just trying to figure out all the things I've had to navigate. I'll be picking you from now on, and I know so many other people who will feel the same way. Heck, I might even drive from Big Rapids just to visit your shop," I replied. I knew I was basically on my high horse. I felt like a professor pontificating about their area of expertise. My confidence surprised me.

"You both might be right," Frank uttered. I could tell he wanted to join the buy-in. His heart was yelling at him to do it, but his mind was lagging. Hopefully, we'd given his mind enough comfort to assuage his fears and let his heart take the lead. I could also tell we shouldn't push it any further. We planted the seeds.

"Well, Zach will be back soon, and we have to get back to work."

"I know it's a difficult choice," I said. "And we will always be here to talk more if you want."

"You're just kids, and you are so brave," he uttered. "You've given me a lot to think about. You'll be hearing from me."

"Take your time to think it through," I continued. "And remember, if Tim or Zach ever need anything, we are here."

"I will," Frank said. "Thank you for coming to see me."

"Of course, thank you for thinking about joining the campaign," David said. "Even the fact you're thinking about it and reached out shows we're making an impact."

"You are," Frank uttered as we started leaving. "More than you could know"

A few moments later, David and I found ourselves back in Common Grounds; the line seemed as long as ever. David said, "I think that went well. I sort of want to send him another picture of how long this line is."

"I honestly don't think we need to," I replied. "I think we convinced him."

"You think so?" David asked. "I don't know. He seemed very indecisive."

"Oh, he was," I exclaimed. "But I think he'll follow his heart."

"Maybe? I guess I'm so used to debating; following one's heart isn't really a thing," David laughed.

"I guess time will tell," I smiled.

"Guess so," he replied. "So, what do you need to work on today?"

The line slowly moved forward as I answered, "I need to figure out my life. I still have no idea what my major should be."

"I might be a bit biased, but have you thought about taking a debate class?" David gave an exaggerated wink.

I chuckled and exclaimed, "We'll have to see about that, too. I have been thinking more about how I want to be a public advocate and everything."

"You're a natural. How many other folks can say they've already given a speech in front of the City Council?" David continued. And, with that, I think his cute little joke about it solidified a vague idea into a goal.

"You might be right," I said, now the second in line.

"And, who else has already been to the Capital to protest for a more just criminal justice system?" He was laying it on thick now.

"Not many people, I take it," I answered.

"Nope," he said as he turned to the barista. "I'll have a large hot toasted marshmallow latte."

And that was that. We didn't talk about me taking a debate class for the rest of the day. But I kept thinking about what he had said as I looked for potential classes next year. Could I succeed in debate class?

The next morning, I got a huge injection of confidence when I got a message from Gloria. "You need to check the campaign page. We've been tagged by another business. They are joining the campaign!"

I immediately looked up the post on social media. It was Frank. I excitedly texted Gloria back, "David and I talked with him yesterday!"

"Great work!" Gloria responded.

I read and re-read the post, "At Frank's Automotive Repair, we don't care what you drive, who you are, or who you love. We just want to provide you with high-quality service, and we want to ensure you're safe on the road. We'll never deny you service based on your race, ethnicity, age, religion, sex, or sexual orientation. Because we believe that all businesses should be open to everyone, we will be supporting the Love Triumphs campaign."

The post already had over one hundred likes, about thirty comments, and several shares. Frank was active in thanking people for their support, and Zach liked all the affirming comments. I imagined they made a few more customers that day, just as David had predicted.

David! I had to let him know the great news.

"We did it!" I texted. "Frank just posted he's joining!"

"Terrific!" David texted me back. "We should get together and celebrate with everyone! A win is a win!"

"Sounds great!" I replied.

"We make sure a great team!" He texted back.

"Yes, we do!" I agreed.

Session #37

"Here's to us!" Gloria exclaimed, raising her glass of water for a toast. We had decided to meet at Little Rapids Bistro for lunch to celebrate Frank's decision to join our campaign. Thankfully, Gloria and Herald agreed to pay; otherwise, I doubt I could have gone. Seriously, we need to get another affordable option to join the buy-in.

We all clinked glasses. It was a smaller group than I hoped, but I knew others were busy. School was ending, so Naomi had a lot of homework. Pastor Esther had some denominational meeting to prepare for. Ruth told me the meeting was expected to be controversial because they had to discuss some incidents of racism in other churches.

Because of all that, it was just me, David, Ruth, Gloria, and Herald. A small but formidable team.

Gloria and Herald were already seated when the rest of us showed up. They ordered various flatbreads for the table as the appetizer, but honestly, they could have been the main course. They were massive.

After our toast, we started chatting about the buy-in campaign and our next steps. Ruth commented, "We are moving in the right direction, so I say we just keep doing what we are doing. We just keep talking with people about joining the campaign, and we keep up the pressure on businesses."

"And let people know about our successes," David exclaimed. "Frank's saying he's never had so much business?"

"Yeah, people have been coming from Big Rapids to go to his little shop," I added. "He might even need to hire another mechanic."

"I'll touch up my resume," Herald joked.

"But, seriously, I'm so proud of what we've accomplished so far," Gloria said.

"Me too." I felt the muscles around my mouth working to stop my smile from becoming a manic grin.

"This has been an answer to so many prayers," David interjected. "I prayed for so many nights that something like this would happen."

A tear worked its way down David's face. I felt all of it: the sadness of it taking this long, all the memories of longing and praying for a better day, the pure joy of finally doing something about it, the excitement that we could have a more inclusive town, and the epiphany discovering we were the answer to our prayers. David uttered, "Sorry, I told myself I wasn't going to cry."

"You don't need to be sorry," Gloria instantly stated.

"I get it," I said. "It all feels so… surreal."

"It feels good, doesn't it?" Ruth asked.

"It does," David replied. "After all the waiting and all the praying and all the despair and darkness, it feels like seeing the sunrise for the first time."

"It is a new day here in Small Rapids," I exclaimed.

"That it is," David concurred. "I know we still have a lot of work to do, but I'm happy. I'm optimistic."

"Don't lose hope, David," Ruth instructed.

We sat for a moment, letting it all in. Herold interrupted the silence, "I'm just very proud of this group."

"Me too," Gloria agreed.

We sat chatting for over two hours. For a long time, I've felt as if I couldn't do small talk. But I felt at ease with these people. David shared about the final projects he was working on for his classes, and so did I. Ruth shared that she had been reading more about scripture and disability. Gloria was thinking about changing up her garden and trying to grow pumpkins. Herald was volunteering for a local program teaching kids woodshop. My heart felt as full as my stomach, which was stuffed.

Eventually, David announced, "Well, I better go work on my final projects."

"I should, too," I agreed.

"School's ending pretty soon, isn't it?" Ruth asked.

"In like two weeks," I replied. "I can't believe it. It went by so fast."

"I have way too much to work on," David exclaimed. "I need to work on my procrastination."

"I'm sure you will do fine," Gloria said. "You always do."

"Thanks, Gloria," David replied.

A few moments later, David and I found ourselves in the parking lot. As he pivoted toward his car, he looked at me and said, "Meet at Common Grounds?"

"Sounds good," I replied.

Session #38

HI AARON,

I've been so excited to share this with you—about my conversation with David at Common Grounds. I need to admit I was unprepared for it, and it caught me off guard. But I feel like it will be for the better.

We ordered our normal drinks and sat in what was beginning to feel like our normal spot. But, before I had a chance to start working on one final essay that needed to be around fifteen pages long, David started the conversation.

"Please don't laugh at me," David said with a hint of nervous energy. What was he worried about?

"I won't! I promise." I answered firmly, finding it a bit difficult to believe he would think I would ever laugh at him.

"Well, I was wondering if you wanted to get dinner with me sometime?" he continued. I had never felt him be this tense. I could feel his anxiety so clearly, and it felt like my skin was crawling. And then... it dawned on me.

"Like, on a date?" I asked hesitantly, praying I was reading the situation correctly.

"Yeah, that's what I was thinking, but totally forget I said anything if you don't want to," he answered.

"I'd love to," I exclaimed.

"Really?" he said as the tension dissipated.

"Yes, really," I answered. "But don't get your hopes up. I haven't been on a date in a long time."

I joked about it, but I think I was a bit nervous. As you know, I've never been all the way with someone. It's been a while since I dated, and Mario and I were never open about our relationship. I imagine David would want to be open about ours. Would he have to wait for marriage to do it? Then I caught myself and reined myself in. My mind was racing ahead, coming up with scenario after scenario, until my anxiety prevented me from taking the first step. It was just a date, one date.

He laughed, "Don't worry. I'll go easy on you."

"Thanks," I replied. "What did you have in mind?"

"Well, if I'm going easy on you. What about just dinner and a movie?" he said.

"Sounds perfect," I answered.

"Well, I guess the Bistro it is, unless we want to go somewhere in Big Rapids," David exclaimed with a sly smirk on his face.

"Big Rapids sounds wonderful," I replied.

And I smiled; it was Mario's smile, at least I would like to think it was. It had been such a long time since I felt this sense of a warm glow radiating in me. I thought any minute, I might start floating. My joy could not be contained by gravity. Was this moment bittersweet for me? Yes, of course. But it felt sweeter. I know Mario would want me to be happy, and he would want me to move on. And I felt something with David that I had not felt in a long time: safe. It was the same way I felt with the people at Central Street United Methodist Church, too. Now, I feel safe for the first time in a long time, and I know I can continue healing and reach my full potential once again.

Session #39

Hey Aaron,

I imagine you've figured it out by now, but I want to talk a little bit more about what happened on the day of the shooting. I've told you about some of it, but not everything. We always said I should only share what I am comfortable sharing when I'm comfortable sharing it.

I think I'm ready now.

I still remember the screams in the distance coming closer and closer; some days, they still echo in my dreams. I still hear the footsteps running down the hall, frantically searching for safety; somedays, I could swear I hear running when no one is around me.

I hear the thud as someone smashes into the library door. The jiggling at the door and the librarian helping him as he enters.

His screams eviscerate me. With every screech, it feels like someone has stabbed me in the stomach. I want to vomit because it hurts so much.

I don't want to look, and I don't at first. I know the horror awaiting me if I look at him.

"We need to stop this bleeding," Ms. Mullen exclaims.

"Too... much," he replies.

I force myself to look. He's collapsed on the ground, and the librarian is kneeling beside him. I know what I'm about to see. I know it's going to be the most painful thing I'll ever have to witness. But I need to see him. I want to help if I can.

I look at his hair first and then at the blood. There is so much blood. I don't think he sees me, but I scramble as quickly as I can from under the desk and crawl toward him. My unconscious mind has taken over, and I start pulling off my shirt. I lean down next to him and, with a swift motion, press my shirt down as hard as I can, where the blood is spilling out of his stomach.

He looks at me. His familiar eyes connect with mine, and I see the life draining from his eyes. The corner of his lips twinges a bit as his smile fights to appear. It never quite makes it; before it can, he's coughing up blood.

I know this is the last time I can utter those three simple yet meaningful words to him. But I freeze. I fight the threatening bile, knowing I could vomit at any moment. I'm gripped by fear; everything in my being wants to tell him I love him. I want to tell him in front of the librarian, my psychology teacher, and the whole class. I desperately want him to hear the words from him. But everything in my being is afraid. We'd made no agreement to tell people, and when we did, we were going to do it together. This wasn't the plan. How can I let those words slip out?

Now, of course, I regret my decision. My choice was to remain silent. I looked him in the eyes, and now I hoped he could feel my love for him.

Even now, I hope he can feel how much I loved him, how much I wanted to kiss him one last time, and how much I cared for him.

I think he sensed it. Within a few moments, he took his last breath. Ms. Mullen and I sat in the pool of his blood, drained. Drained and devoid of emotion, my numbness settled in.

I don't think I processed anything at that point. Somehow, I realized the gunfire was silent. The distant screams were not. Somehow, time figured out how to continue both slow motion where it took me an hour to take a breath and a more rapid pace as everything around me sped up.

I inhaled. The police secured the building.

I exhaled. The school evacuated.

I inhaled. Parents showed up, running to hug their loved ones. At least those who survived.

I exhaled. Grief counselors arrived.

I inhaled. Mario's lifeless body remained next to me until someone dragged me to my feet. They knew we were friends—that we attended a youth group together. I doubt they knew I had just watched the love of my life bleed out in front of me.

I exhaled.

How dare the clock continue to tick when my present has just been ripped apart? How dare the future continue to arrive minute after minute? How dare the earth have the audacity to keep rotating when my world had just bled out on the library floor? How dare the people around me continue to try to live their lives? How dare politicians show up and give speeches as if it was just another day at work? How dare folks continue as normal when I could never imagine having a typical day again?

I still have days where I want to curse the sun for daring to continue its path around this planet, to rise and to set, to bring light and to leave us in darkness.

I still have days where I want time to pause so I can just be in the present. I want to wallow in my misery and hurt; I want to rage and scream and throw things. I want to throw myself on the ground with streaming tears. I still have days where I fear the future and what horror awaits me around the next turn. I worry any happiness I feel is false, dangling there in front of me waiting to get ripped from me once again.

But increasingly, I have days where I feel fresh and new, like a long-extinguished candle that is starting to flicker. I feel like I can turn all my hurt into something to help others. Although the pain still lingers—it's always just below the surface—I realize how blessed I was to know Mario in the first place.

Mario will always be with me, and I will be forever grateful for what I learned from him, how much he loved me, and our beautiful relationship. Maybe it *is* better to love and lose than it is to never love after all?

I finally feel like the fear is leaving me, and what is left is a fierce urgency to make things better—one day at a time. I can make sure that all the many Marios still out there will have a better life, a more fulfilling life; they will find love, kindness, compassion, and community. I want to devote my life to doing the same.

I know there are still a lot of Marios struggling with discrimination for who they are and how they love. We have a lot of work to do to craft caring and loving communities; I know there's plenty of work ahead.

So, I do not want to say this is a happy ending. After all, it's not really an ending; it's a new beginning, right? I guess only time will tell how everything turns out. For now, I know I am feeling better, more hopeful, and more alive. I want to get up in the morning and face a new day. I haven't always wanted to do that.

This is how I can honor Mario and the other fourteen. I can live my life to the fullest and cherish every moment I have. I can wake up every day and love others. I can wake up every day and let my positive light radiate to those around me, infectiously smiling wherever I go. I can wake up every day and show kindness and compassion to those in need. I can shelter and aid those buffeted by the harshness of the world. I can be the light Mario, and I always wanted and needed. And I plan on doing just that for as long as I can.

Thanks to you, I am looking forward to what is next, cautiously optimistic that I will have a more loving future and that we can and will build a more beautiful world. I desperately want to live life again. I'm excited for what awaits me. And I am forever grateful you took the time to listen and let me get it all out. You saved me. I hope I can return the favor and save someone else someday.

Thank you from the bottom of my heart.

Love Always,

Jason.

About the Author

I'm Vico Black, a gay neurodivergent storyteller and content creator. Stores are powerful. They entertain, motivate, and inspire. My aim is to write engaging, authentic novels to bring joy, healing, and hope.

My passion is creating young adult coming of age stories about sexuality, faith, and mental health. When I've not writing, I enjoy cuddling with my dachshund, rewatching television shows, and playing video games.

I'd love to get to know you, so please send me an email at authorvicoblack@gmail.com or follow me on Instagram (authorvicoblack) if you want to connect or have feedback for me!

For finishing *Dear My Therapist*, please enjoy a free novella about Jason's experience in a mental health facility by visiting https://vicoblack.wordpress.com

I greatly appreciate you and your support.